THE BILLIONAIRE'S PLAYGROUND

BILLIONAIRE'S
Muse

JP SAYLE

Book Cover © 2021 Design by Tina Løwén
People in images are models and should not be connected to the characters in the book. Any resemblance is incidental.

Editing by Guy Cornelius
Proofreading Abbie Nicole
Book Formatting by Tina Løwén

References to real people, events, organisations, locations, or establishments are only intended to give a sense of authenticity and have been used fictitiously.

The author acknowledges the copyrighted or trademarked status and trademark of any goods, Grindr.

Films, music, and lyrics mentioned are the property of the copyright holders.

Warning
Some of the content of this book is sexually graphic, with the use of explicit language and adult situations involving two males. It is only intended for mature audiences.

STORY OUTLINE

A body resembling a string, no filter, and a waffle to word ratio causes confusion. None of that seems to matter to Marcus. Will he last the distance when it comes to loving Finlo?

When world-renowned photographer, Marcus Crestwell, agreed to do a favour for a friend, he thought it would be a boring photoshoot, but it's anything but. When he meets Agnes, aka Nanna, and Finlo, the laughter that has been missing from his life returns, thanks to the antics of interfering women and a man who is fast becoming irresistible every time he opens his mouth.

Finlo Denning's mind is a lot like spaghetti junction, on a good day. He often finds it hard to stop whatever is in there from spilling right out of his mouth. This means people don't stick around for long. That is until Nanna and Marcus show up. All Finlo has to do now is survive an interfering Nanna with good intentions, to claim Marcus's love. What could possibly go wrong?

Billionaire's Muse, book three in the Billionaire's Playground series, is a light-hearted gay romance with a quirky guy, a hot as hell photographer, and a Nanna who always knows best.

For every reader who picks up one of my books and finds themselves transported into my head, your welcome. And remember we all know a Nanna 😊

PROLOGUE

Marcus

Indescribable scents, impossible to capture on film, added to the horror of the view in front of me. Not for the first time today, I asked why I did this to myself, why I continued to put myself through this purgatory.

I blinked twice, the child that had been laughing mere minutes ago, now lying broken, with unseeing eyes. Those eyes seemed to capture my soul and tear a piece of it from my body. Pain for the dead was something I'd never learnt to deal with. These people didn't deserve to die in this way, lying in a pool of fly-infested blood.

Who deserved that, and for what?

The sounds of gunfire weren't unusual, but being so close, the bullet whizzing past my head? That was new. I'd known it was stupid to get in closer just to capture the child laughing. Her laughing face had depicted the truth, that living in hell didn't mean there was no hope, no joy.

Then the bastards had stolen that from her. My vision blurred, and I blinked furiously, fighting past my own emotions to capture the picture. This child needed their story told. Those monsters shouldn't get away with these atrocities. This was for the casualties, so they wouldn't be forgotten in the political agenda of war that left a country desolate.

The light above the bombed-out building framed the backdrop, with hues of deep purples that cast an almost grey shadow over what was once most likely home to the child.

More children's cries were followed by screams as people ran from the ensuing chaos the mortar attack had caused. I took a deep, shaky breath and clicked the shutter on my camera, capturing the misery, the deprivation, the carnage of a war that no one could fully understand unless they'd lived and breathed it.

These people, hiding in the dusty, scattered ruins of their demolished homes, were the ones that the world's media should be focusing on, not the political wrangling being used to try to justify this. It was a fucking disgrace, and as I moved to lower my camera, I knew at that moment, I couldn't do this any longer. That if I continued, I wasn't sure there would be anything left inside me but the black sucking hole of self-destruction. It seemed the world I'd chosen to immortalise was nothing more than death's gruesome playground.

Ten years, ten years of capturing the world's atrocities was more than enough. As the thought registered, mortar fire rained down on a building no more than thirty feet from me, spewing concrete in every direction as it erupted. I cursed under my breath. Sweat dripped into my eyes as I ducked behind the remnants of a wall, my arse hitting the ground hard.

Huge chunks of rubble dug into my jeans, the sharp edges trying to break through the thick material.

"Marcus, for fuck's sake, are you okay?" called Steve from the direction of where I'd left him cowering the second I'd mentioned I wanted to take several more pictures before we headed out of hell. He'd been my assistant from when I'd started out, and I could hear the genuine fear in his voice over the chaos going on around me.

"If you're not dead, then you're gonna be in ten seconds if you don't fucking answer me."

"Keep your hair on, Steve, I'm okay," I shouted back, not because I thought the seven stone weakling could actually kick my arse, more because I didn't want him getting his arse shot at if he decided to come and find me. We'd become friends over the years, and I knew he had my back.

Inching to the edge of the wall, it was hard to see past the plume of concrete dust to check where the shooters were. I inhaled deeply, regretting it when dust filled my lungs and I had to fight the urge to cough. Holding on to my camera, I used my other hand to pull up the scarf hanging around my neck to cover my lower face. Working on trying not to cough up a lung, I did a countdown in my head.

Steadier, I peeked out to check where I was going to run and what I could use as a shield. A second later, I was up and darting in between jagged bits of building. They definitely wouldn't shield a six-foot-three guy like me, not in my wildest dreams, so I tried hard not to think about how exposed I was. I didn't exhale until I rounded the building where I'd left Steve.

"Thank fuck," Steve said the second I appeared. "Why the fuck do you do this to me? I've aged twenty years in the last two minutes, I'm sure of it."

I shook my head, working on trying to lighten the situation for both of us. "Give over. You've always looked like an old fucker." He hadn't. He was three years younger than my thirty-six, but some days, like now, he looked

8

older than me, with the deep lines etched into his face.

"Ha fucking ha. Get your gear. We need to get out of here, now. That was far too fucking close for comfort. My job is to assist you, not get my arse shot at."

His genuine fear stopped me from coming back with a flippant response. He liked to bitch and complain, but he didn't often get spooked. Pale cheeks and eyes that wheeled around as he spoke told me this had been a 'come to Jesus' moment he'd not wanted.

Quickly packing my camera back into its bag, I slung it over my shoulder. Steve was ready to go and motioned for me to follow before he took off at a sprint in the opposite direction to the gun and mortar fire. Being that much lighter than me, he was a lot faster.

I dug deep in my reserve tank and upped my pace to keep up with him. Years of working out did little in fifty-degree heat while wearing a flak jacket that felt like a fifty-pound rucksack strapped to my chest.

Sweat drenched my shirt, and it rubbed against my skin, leaving it raw by the time the jeep came into view. We'd borrowed it from the guy at the airfield for a princely sum. I could have bought the thing brand new for cheaper. This one looked fit for the knackers yard, but I'd handed over my cash, knowing how much these people needed it. I made a mental note to get Jed, my mother's personal assistant, to ensure the families in the village, which was now no more than rubble, were added to the foundation's allocation of funding. It would never replace their loved ones, and that was the bit I'd come to loath, but it would help them gain some of their life back.

Money. What good was it if you couldn't stop this shit? The number of zeros on my bank balance had meant I could use my cash to help get me to get closer to the action. What it didn't do was take away the reality of what was happening in the world.

Years ago, I'd been naive when I'd first started out taking photos in places like this. I'd seen the shot, the image, but not the impact on the location or the people. I'd been wrapped up in my own self-importance and getting the perfect picture. That had waned very fast. It was a child, much like the one I'd captured today, that had changed that for me.

The small boy had been sitting on the step outside his home. It looked as if he'd been playing with a battered-looking car when, for some reason I couldn't fathom, he'd been shot in the head and had fallen back against the door. From the left side, he looked like he was simply resting until I'd moved just a fraction and brought him into focus. The right side of his face had been partially missing. Dried blood covered his right shoulder, flaking down onto his chubby legs, making him look like one of the Halloween characters from a scary movie. I'd taken a shot from both angles, and when I developed the film, I cried at the cruelty of life.

Coming from a privileged background, where I'd been able to have every whim met, money had shielded me from the hard truths of the world. That little boy had taken my reality and shown me that money meant nothing if it couldn't protect the weak, the innocent. From that moment, something had changed inside me that was reflected in my work. Someone once wrote that I used my heart, not my eyes, to take pictures. I wasn't sure it was that, at least not fully. To me, it was the heart of the person I wanted to capture.

I stumbled to a halt a few seconds after Steve, who was already getting in the jeep, appearing none the worse for our jog. My chest burned as I sucked in air through the scarf covering my mouth.

Steve sat in the driver's seat and switched on the engine. "Get in. Come on, stop pissing about." He didn't even appear winded as he spoke.

I got in, my chest continuing to heave as I placed my camera bag in the footwell. Using the scarf covering my lower face, I wiped the sweat from my skin. Suddenly, the jeep shot forward and jerked over the rocky ground. I bounced up and whacked my head on the roof. "Fucking hell! Give me a chance to buckle up."

"Not a fucking chance. That was far too close for comfort." Steve never took his eyes off what had once been a road but now was more like a dirt track with giant boulders scattered across it.

I reached for the seat belt with one hand while holding on to the dashboard with the other to try and prevent my now throbbing head from making contact with the metal again.

"Why can't you be like any normal person and choose to take pictures of fucking flowers or...something," Steve demanded.

I snorted. "Because I've never been a follower."

"Well, this follower is quitting the second we get on the plane out of here."

The fear was tangible in the confines of the jeep. "You know you've told me that nine times over the years?"

His gaze shifted to me briefly, a deep vee appearing between his brows. "I fucking mean it this time. I'm too old for this shit. 'Steve, I've a great opportunity for you, come work for me'. Great opportunity to get your arse shot at more like."

He mimicked me to perfection, and for the first time in days, a smile tugged at the corner of my lips. "What's not great about this life?" I said in his northern accent.

"You're not fucking funny, so stop talking."

The whiteness of his knuckles as he clung to the steering wheel got me to shut up and stop distracting him. Long minutes passed as Steve drove us towards the bit of ground that professed to be a private landing strip, but in reality was just a bit of open land someone had fenced off.

The sounds of the mortar attacks lessened with each mile he drove, yet I still didn't breathe easy.

"Is the plane ready to take off the second we get there?" Steve asked, breaking the silence after several minutes.

"It is. I asked Hal to have everything ready for a quick escape. You did the research on the private landing strip. Do you think we'll encounter any issues?" The thing about countries like this one? Their governments didn't want the outside world to see what was really happening. I'd had my equipment taken in the past. I'd quickly learnt to remove the film from the camera and replace it with shots that wouldn't arouse too much suspicion if they developed the photos.

I reached for the camera bag when I realised in my haste to escape, I'd not changed out the spool. A minute later, the camera was back in the bag, and I'd tucked the reel into a pocket that was hidden inside my clothing. I'd had special pockets inserted into my trousers that weren't obvious, in areas a normal search wouldn't normally check.

"I triple checked this place, and the money I handed over should keep the guy quiet...hopefully."

He didn't sound all that convinced as he drew to a stop outside the ten-foot-tall, barbed-wire gates. The small, private airfield housed one building that looked more like an outhouse than a control tower.

There was a helicopter and one plane, which looked as if it would fall apart the second it tried to take off, tucked off to the left side of the building. The sleek-looking jet that I owned was so out of place it was almost funny.

I sighed.

The thing had been purchased for one purpose. To get me in and out of countries fast after I'd learnt I didn't like to be detained and questioned about what I was up to. My mother had not been best pleased to find herself having to bail me out of tricky situations, using her power and influence to get my arse out of jail. I'd not been too happy about the situation either, to be honest. My mother and I didn't see eye to eye on my choice of career before that. After that...well, we didn't talk about it.

The man we'd met when we landed six hours earlier appeared from the shack. His clothes were threadbare, and his hair was badly in need of a cut. The beard was scruffy, and I was sure it contained bits of food. He hadn't given us his name. He was only interested in the cash we'd offered to land here.

The sound of metal grinding on metal was deafening, even with the windows of the jeep closed. The rusty gates groaned in what sounded like relief when they clanged against the metal posts that stopped it from hitting the fence. "Quick, quick," the man shouted, motioning to us.

I glanced over my shoulder, half-convinced I'd see an army chasing us. I didn't breathe any easier when I saw nothing but the dirt road we'd travelled on and the baron, rocky land covered in a shimmering heat haze.

"Quick, quick," he repeated after Steve parked inside the gates.

"Do you think he knows any other words?" Steve asked, his dry sense of humour appearing to have returned now we were back at the plane.

"Possibly not, but let's not ask right now. He seems to know something we don't."

Exactly five minutes later, Hal taxied down the dirt strip, and we were sailing up in the air. I glanced down at the land beneath, feeling the weight of the camera spool pressing against my leg. Bone deep weariness followed.

I was done with this life.

I blew out a breath and looked back at Steve. "Contact Sigrid and tell her I can do the photoshoot she was after me doing for her."

Steve's relief came quick, then the humour. "You know she's not going to give you a minute's peace the second I contact her."

I gave a heartfelt sigh and looked back out at the ruined land below. "It'll be better than this. That's all that matters right now."

CHAPTER ONE

Marcus

My mother's brow never moved, the Botox doing its job as she raised her gaze from the computer screen to me. "Why would I be interested in a college fashion project?"

"Because your one and only son thinks it's going to be an event you'll enjoy. Charlie and Guy are two inspirational men who are looking to design clothing for real-sized people. They want to help them feel good about their bodies."

When Charlie had reached out to ask if I'd be interested in photographing the event, I'd been sure I was going to turn him down, but then he'd invited me to his home. I'd accepted the offer because he lived with Griffin, his partner, and my long-time friend. I didn't get to see Griffin often, or I hadn't, back when I'd spent so much time out of England. That was changing, though with Griffin's current schedule, he was harder to pin down than me these days. I'd been more than happy to go for dinner, and it turned out the talk about the venture had left me intrigued enough to agree to photograph the event. It also didn't hurt my ego that Charlie was a fan of my work.

I was charmed by Charlie's beliefs about how designer clothes should be made to fit a person's personality and body shape to help them feel good about themselves. It was a bold concept in today's fashion market, which was why I'd come to see my mother, who was always looking for something that she could invest in. Despite her scepticism, I could see this being a good fit.

Only thing was, I needed to see if I could prise her away from her desk. To say she was a workaholic was an understatement and all because of the death of my father. My dad had been bitten by a tick on holiday, which had resulted in him becoming unwell. They'd come home early, only it was too late. Several days later, all his organs failed, and they'd turned off his life support machine. It had been a shock, one my mother had never recovered from. Fifteen years later, she was still buried in the empire they'd built together, hiding from what I'd accepted; he wasn't going to come back through the door, larger than life, a beaming smile on his face.

It hurt my heart that I'd not lost just my dad but had, in essence, lost my mother too.

"I've told you before, mind reading isn't in my repertoire. I'll ask again, why would I be interested in this?" Her brow remained smooth, even as one eyebrow moved a millimetre up. The hint of impatience, which was never far away, was present in the snap of her tone, even if her expression couldn't fully show it.

I got up and came around the desk, leaning down to kiss her scented cheek. "You'll enjoy it. Come for me, please?"

She didn't so much as move a muscle, but I sensed her acceptance even before her head moved, and she stared at me with onyx eyes, identical to mine. "You're so much like your father." The sadness came and went so fast it could fool me into believing I'd not seen it until she cupped my cheek and squeezed. "I'll come, but only for half an hour."

I grinned. "I'll take whatever I can get. I'll have Steve send Jed the details for the event. It's at The Worthington."

"Is Griffin going?" The only way I could tell she was frowning was by a tiny wrinkle between her brows. It was very disconcerting.

The Worthington was one of the many hotels that Griffin Hudson owned. "He is.

Griffin is dating Charlie," I said, unable to resist dropping that little tidbit, knowing it would get a rise out of her.

She didn't disappoint as her voice rose several octaves. "What? Griffin is...straight, isn't he?" The wrinkle deepened the tiniest of fractions.

I chuckled. "Not that straight, it would seem."

Sigrid, a designer I loved dearly, asked me to do a fashion shoot for her a few months back. Griffin, it turned out, was the financial backer for Sigrid's new range of men's lingerie. It was also when I'd first met Charlie and where Griffin had turned up, getting in my face when he thought I was hitting on the boy. At the time, I'd kept my surprise to myself but hadn't been able to resist winding him up. He'd always seemed a little too closed off for his own good.

That I was gay and Charlie was dressed in nothing but sexy underwear had made Griffin an easy target. Charlie was attractive, but he just wasn't my type, not that I really had a type. Well, not in a long time. Dating had not been something I'd been interested in. Being out of the country a lot of the time, I was more of a fucking and having fun kinda guy. Now I was home on a more permanent basis, I wasn't sure whether I'd be looking to change that or not. The last few months, I'd not even bothered with Grindr for a hook-up.

"It's all very…sudden."

"I'm not sure it's that sudden, but they're a couple now. Griffin has bought a house in Brighton, not far from that new investment property you bought."

"How do you know that?"

I tapped the side of my head. "I do read the reports you get Jed to send me every quarter. I might not want to take over your empire, but that doesn't mean I'm not interested, Mum. I've told you this before."

It was an old argument, one I tried not to get into as neither of us ever came out of the conversation feeling satisfied. No matter how many times I explained this business was not for me, it never got past the barrier she'd erected to stop hearing me.

"Jed invites you to all the board meetings too."

I shook my head. "Not happening. I'm not wasting my life sitting in a stuffy room with stuffy men and women talking boring crap."

"That boring crap pays the bills you run up." Her tone was sharp enough to cut.

"It pays none of my bills, and you know it. That money goes to good causes. To people that need the money more than we do," I gritted out through clenched teeth, working on controlling the temper that had no place between us.

She ran a hand over her styled, silver-flecked hair, the only sign of her agitation.

"That was uncalled for. I'm sorry." I heaved out a sigh. "Let's drop it. I'll send Jed the information and some dates for us to do dinner next week."

I gave her a hard hug, one she returned. "I love you."

"Same. Now go on with you. I'm busy."

I chuckled, letting her go. "See you next week."

I left to go talk to Jed. He looked up and gave me a distracted smile I was used to. The man always seemed to be doing ten jobs at once. He raised his finger, indicating for me to wait for a second while he wrote something down on a piece of paper.

Only when his gaze moved back to me did I speak. "I'll be sending you some information for a fashion show that's happening next week. Can you make sure it's in Mum's calendar?"

His eyes gleamed. "She's agreed to go?"

I grinned, knowing he'd understand what a big thing it was for my mother to break from her routine. "Yep, but only after I twisted her arm." A thought popped into my head. "I could send you a ticket too. You can bring her and make sure she doesn't leave after ten minutes...have some fun away from the office?"

The colour that appeared to flood his cheeks confirmed what I'd suspected for a long time. Jed was a man in his fifties and was, as far as I knew, single. I'd come to wonder if his single status might be because he'd feelings for my mother. The man worked harder than ten horses pulling a huge wagon. He was always here with my mother.

Had she noticed? Possibly.

Was it my business? No.

Did that mean I wasn't going to interfere?

I eyed the man in front of me and gave him a little nudge. "They have a lovely restaurant in the hotel. I could book a table for all of us?" What I meant was for them two, but I left that part out.

"I'm sure your mother would like that...I mean to eat with you...not me."

Letting him off the hook, I winked. "I get it. But I'm sure you're wrong about her only enjoying eating with me." With that, I gave him a wide grin and a nod before heading out.

I waited till I was in the lift to laugh at the bewildered smile I'd left him with. It was time they got their act together. It really was.

Life was far too fucking short to waste it.

Lifeless eyes stared back at me, and I closed my eyes, the laughter dying.

CHAPTER TWO

Fin

Minding my own business, I was surprised to see Guy and Charlie heading towards me. They were striking to look at, and I got why Charlie had his face plastered all over magazines. The guy was a model, as well as a student, and extremely hot, in that nerdy kind of way.

"Fin, I've been looking for you," Guy said as he came to a stop in front of me.

I held up the sandwich I'd been enjoying on the grassy bank not far from the main building at Brighton uni. "I'm here," I answered, eliciting a frown from Guy.

"Yeah, I see that," Guy replied. "Have you heard that we're putting on a fashion show?"

Guy pointed between him and Charlie, but Charlie wasn't paying any attention to us. He was busy staring at his phone, scowling.

"Someone mentioned it. That's great for the pair of you." My major was in history. Understanding what had come before us had made history an easy choice, especially as I loved researching the past and imagining what life had been like. What I was going to do with my degree once I was finished, I'd yet to figure out.

"We came up with the great idea to use students to wear our clothes to show off the versatility of them."

Smiling, my head tried to come up with a reason as to why Guy was telling me all this.

"—so, would you be interested?"

He'd carried on talking, but I'd got lost somewhere along the way. It wasn't uncommon. I stared at the man in front of me, scratching at the side of my head. "Guy, you need to say that again. I think I missed a bit. There's no way you're asking me to be in your fashion show?" I made a point of glancing down my body that resembled something akin to a wet noodle...although that may have been an insult to noodles. The old baggy combat trousers and ripped hoodie I'd found in a charity shop did little to disguise how thin I was.

A fashion show, me? It was laughable, if not a little dangerous for anyone who got too close to my uncontrollable limbs. With a mum who was all about love, peace, and light, I'd been homeschooled. The school she'd sent me to originally had tried to, in her words, "pigeonhole me to fit one of their boxes," though I'd no clue what that meant. All I understood was that I had an excess of energy that left me ultra-skinny.

Though, that didn't account for a brain that ran faster than the speed of light. This often left my mouth without the ability to change gears and keep whatever was in my head from spilling right out, like verbal diarrhea.

Guy's grin widened. "You heard me right. I want you to be in the show. You're gorgeous, and this is about showing how body shape doesn't define beauty."

"That's flattering, but have you seen me in action? I'm all arms and legs and have the coordination of a baby giraffe...only without the long neck...and legs. I mean, I'd look stupid with those and a small body."

I shook my head, trying to stop my mouth from voicing all that was going on inside my head. "Thanks, it was nice of you to offer, man."

"So that's a yes then?" Guy asked, looking more than a little confused.

"I...suppose?" Had I said yes?

"Great, we are having a fitting at Charlie's house tonight. Can you make it?"

There was never much in my calendar other than study. I'd a few friends on campus, but I was tiring to most people, so they tended to only want to spend minimal time with me. I got it. I tired myself sometimes. "Should be fine. Can you send me the address?"

Three minutes later, both men walked off, and I finished my sandwich, trying to figure out how I was going to not let either man down.

I shrugged. I had warned them.

The house in front of me was large and...expensive. I'd heard the rumours that Charlie had nabbed himself a billionaire, but I wasn't one to gossip or poke my nose into other people's business, so I'd not paid much attention. The door in front of me opened, and I blinked twice, trying to recall if I'd pressed the bell.

A woman in her late seventies, possibly eighties, appeared. She stopped and gave me a head to toe look before an impish smile formed on her pretty face. "You must be Fin."

"That's me," I said with an answering smile, "and you are?"

"I'm Agnes, but you can call me Nanna."

"Nanna, where the heck are you?" Charlie's voice floated out of the door from somewhere behind Nanna, sounding frustrated.

"Charlie boy, why do you always have to shout?" she called, back loud enough to make my ears ring.

He appeared a second later, rolling his eyes and giving me a sympathetic smile. "I'm going to apologise now for anything that comes out of Nanna's mouth. And be warned, if she gives you anything to eat or drink, take it with caution."

"One time! One time he takes pills, pills that he asked for, I might add, and it's all my fault he passed out cold after flirting with Griff," she answered, a spark of what looked like mischief in her eyes.

Instantly, I warmed to the woman. "I'm sure Nanna was just being helpful."

Charlie pointed at me. "Don't be fooled by the grandma exterior."

"I'll have less of that, laddie. Do you see a grandma exterior?" she demanded as she glanced at me.

Taking the question seriously, I took in her outfit.

The top was a soft wool polo neck, which elongated her own neck in a baby pink colour that complimented her skin tone. The navy trousers were slim-fitting, and she'd matched them with a bright green pair of flats that were more luminescent than I'd have expected for someone of her age. Her hair was silver-grey and cut into a chic bob that was layered onto her face, highlighting her cheekbones. "In my opinion, I'd say you look a cross between Jane Fonda and Judi Dench. Chic and trendy enough to be a classic, but not at all like an old fashioned grandma."

"He's a keeper," Agnes said, linking her arm through mine and dragging me bodily into the house.

"Nanna! Nanna, come back. Where are you taking Fin?" Charlie called after us.

"To meet Rachael and Cissy," she replied, which meant nothing to me, but I didn't miss Charlie's hissing breath.

Nanna patted my arm. "We're going to have so much fun, you and me. Now tell me a little about yourself."

"Erm, well, what do you want to know?" I asked, a slight quiver in my voice. Nobody ever really wanted to know about me, I'm not very interesting.

She stopped at the end of the hallway and released my arm to reach for the door in front of her. "Let's start with, do you like cats?"

"Don't do it," came a deep, masculine voice from behind me.

I glanced over my shoulder and sucked in a breath at the handsome man dressed in a suit standing not more than two feet away. He was commanding and more than a little intimidating as his eyes narrowed on Nanna and me.

Nanna gave him a smile I was starting to love. It was full of spirit and sass. "Griff, I've no clue what you're talking about. Have you met Fin? He's a lovely boy. He's going to be in the fashion show with us."

"You're going to be in the show too?" This was great news. "That's fantastic," I enthused.

"I am, and it is. I knew I had a good feeling about you."

"Nanna."

"Griff," she answered, then opened the door and all but shoved me through it. "I'll see you in a bit."

The door closed behind her, and she gave me another of those cheeky smiles. "Now, cats, do you like them? Cissy can be a bit of a handful and isn't great when she's hungry."

As if to prove the point, a large ginger tabby cat appeared and made a growling noise, baring its sharp teeth.

"Fucking feed me," came a demonic voice.

I jerked and glanced from the cat to Nanna.

She shrugged. "Cissy has such a foul mouth, be warned."

"I can see that. Maybe we should feed her?" I answered, loving my new friends. I was going to fit right in here. I could see it. "I've a hamster. He's a little tricky too. Maybe I need to train him to talk? What do you think?"

Her laughter made her rock back and forth. A minute later, she wiped at her eyes. "Laddie, if you were only a few years older, I'd keep you."

"Nanna, I'm flattered, but I swing for the other team," I answered regretfully.

"Then we'll settle for being friends." With that, she threaded her arm through mine and was back to dragging me through an archway into a gorgeous room with a view of the beach laid out in front of us.

"I'd like that," I said. And I meant it.

CHAPTER THREE

Marcus

The studio I had on the lower floor of the building that I lived in was seldom used. I tended to only do photoshoots here when I was running short of time. In the main, it was my preference to work in someone else's space, allowing me to separate work from my home. Steve liked to use the lower floor office to work from, said it gave him structure.

I hated structure.

Looking for the man in question, I took the stairs leading down to the studio. "Steve, you here?"

"Where the hell else would I be," he called back from his hunched position, sitting over the computer.

"You need to work on your posture man, your back isn't going to love you in the future."

His hand came up, and he flipped me the bird. "What do you want?"

I chuckled. "Polite, much? I can see why I employed you."

"I'm the only person that will put up with your disorganised arse. Now, why have you come to bother me? Don't you have a fashion shoot to get ready for?" His gaze finally lifted from the screen in front of him, his brows lifting at me.

"That's why I came to find you. Are you planning on staying at The Worthington as well? Griffin has offered everyone a room for the night in the hotel. I'm planning on staying so I don't have to get up at the arse crack of dawn for the dress rehearsal."

"Arse and crack, ha! When was the last time you saw either, at dawn or any other time of day, for that matter?"

"I'm going through a dry spell. What can I say?"

"That you're a pathetic loser?" he replied quickly.

"I could sack you."

He sat back in his seat, a confident grin on his smug face. "You could, but then who would organise all the things you've crammed into your calendar? Who would help at all these photoshoots you've decided to do on top of your already crammed schedule?"

"No one is indispensable," I fired back, trying to add as much threat to my voice as I could.

He laughed long and hard, wiping tears from his eyes. "Good luck with replacing me."

"Cocky fucker."

His grin was contagious. "I tell it how it is, baby."

"Don't let Patrick hear you calling me baby."

He glanced about as if his boyfriend of three years had suddenly appeared in the room. "Tell him I said that, and I'll tell everyone about the guy in Hong Kong."

A little sweaty, I wiped at my top lip. "You wouldn't!"

His eyes narrowed on me. "I would if you tell Patrick I called you baby. You know how he can get."

I did. Steve's boyfriend was the jealous type and overly sensitive. He could very easily get into a state if he thought that Steve was looking at another man. Steve was devoted to Patrick, but was that devotion reciprocated...I wasn't so sure, but I kept my thoughts to myself on the topic.

"You won't be able to use Hong Kong against me forever."

"Watch me. Who gets drunk and asks the biggest guy in the bar if he can do a re-enactment of King Kong with you as the damsel in distress? The pictures alone say a thousand words." His laughter was loud as he leant back fully in the seat, enjoying himself at my expense.

In my defence, the alcohol out there was three times stronger than the booze in England, which I'd found out to my peril. Heat crawled up my neck as I recalled how the guy, who wasn't in the least bit gay or amused, had tried to turn me into a pretzel, and not in a good way. "You show anyone those pictures, and I swear I'll—"

"Offer me a giant pay rise for my amazing skills?" he added through choked laughter.

"I'm already paying you a fucking fortune, so let's just drop this subject and get back to tonight. Are you staying at the hotel?"

He shook his head. "I've plans to take Patrick to a show at the West End that he wants to see, so I'll pass this time. I've got everything ready to take to the hotel. Do you want me to drop you off?"

"That would be great. I'll not need anything, so you don't need to stay." I'd planned to just roam around in the background and take pictures. From my discussion with Charlie and Guy, I hoped it would be enough to capture the energy of the event.

Steve glanced back at the computer. "I should be done in about half an hour. We can go after that if that works?"

"Yeah, that should work. I'll meet you in the garage."

I left him to it, going to pack an overnight bag. A buzz of excitement fizzled to life inside me. The excitement that had been lacking since I'd returned home and developed the shots of the little girl who liked to haunt my dreams. Thoughts followed of the planned exhibition that my agent wanted and I didn't, working to take away the buzz. Pictures I'd taken all those months earlier were still in my development room, and as yet, no one but me had seen them.

I'd signed a contract, one I could easily break if I didn't mind paying a fortune in costs. I could afford it, but the damage to my reputation...maybe not. I ran a hand through my hair as I took the stairs two at a time, leaving the worrying thoughts behind.

Bags packed, I was standing next to Steve's electric car a minute before he arrived. I nodded to the vehicle as he approached. "When did you get this?" The Nissan hybrid looked brand new.

He rolled his eyes. "I told you about this last month when the car dealership said they'd managed to get the colour I wanted."

I kept my face straight as I eyed the cack coloured car. It was a cross between mustard and copper, the colour of baby poo. "It's…*nice*." What could one say about baby poo?

The narrowing of his eyes left me bending to pick up my overnight bag and camera case. "Ready?"

"Yeah…you hate it, don't you?" he asked with resignation.

I gave a shrug. "We all have different tastes. It's why there are so many choices out there." I left it there because Steve could argue the merits of his awful taste for hours once he got started.

In the car and fighting the afternoon traffic, Steve went through the inventory for the next couple of days. "Sigrid needs you to go to hers and go through all the reels of film to help her decide which images she wants to show Griffin."

I laughed. "Griffin might hate all the images."

Steve indicated, switched lanes while cursing at a cyclist who cut in front of him, and then asked, "Why would he hate them? I've seen them. They are beautiful, and the model looks masculine and sexy."

"Exactly. He's also Griffin's boyfriend."

Steve coughed and glanced briefly at me. "How am I only hearing about this now? Griffin is straight, is he not?"

"Was, now he's maybe a little more bent than he first thought. And I never mentioned it because it's not something I think about. I found out at the fashion shoot I did at Sigrid's, the weekend after we came back from that hellish trip that had you deciding to take an impromptu holiday."

"I quit," he replied.

"You say potato, I say tomato. Anyway, Griffin turned up at Sigrid's and made it clear to me that Charlie wasn't in the market for a boyfriend."

"Were you interested?"

"Nah, but you know I can't help winding people up." He rolled his eyes at the windscreen, his mouth pursing. "Griffin was too easy. We're friends. He got over it."

"Lucky for you," he muttered.

I slapped his leg. "You love me. Everyone loves me."

"Yeah, like a hole in the head."

Laughing, I went back to watching the people walking down the streets as Steve drove at a snail's pace through the traffic. I'd missed this. Missed the hustle and bustle of life, where I got to sit back and just watch. It's where I'd found a lot of my inspiration when I was younger. Some of my earlier exhibitions had featured photos that had been taken on these very streets.

Twenty minutes later, I watched Steve pull back into the traffic after leaving me outside The Worthington.

"Can I be of assistance, Sir?" came a voice that sounded like it belonged in a period drama.

I glanced at the guy gussied up in a top hat and tails and grinned, my hand already reaching for my camera bag. "Can I take your picture?"

His eyes widened. "Erm, I'm—"

"Go on."

"Marcus? Marcus, you made it."

I smiled at Charlie, who was rushing towards me, dragging a huge case on wheels behind him. Following him were two other men. Guy, I'd met, blond and cute. He was going to be Charlie's business partner, from what I understood. It was the unknown man that drew my gaze as he struggled to drag another weighty-looking suitcase while two old women chatted next to him. He offered both women a captivating smile. It changed his face entirely.

A smile spread over my face as my head started to see images with shutters of light and shade. The man's dark hair shimmered in the sunlight and showed off the truly awful haircut he had. Yet, there was something about him that pulled at my creative side. My hand started to hurt as my fingers clamped tightly around my camera bag, and I struggled to resist demanding he pose for me right then.

"—will that be all right? I'm not sure what time we're allowed to go in."

"What?" I asked, nonplussed when Charlie gave me a look of expectation. "Were you talking to me?"

His lips quivered, and he glanced at the yet unnamed man, then back to me. "Yeah, I was. I was saying that I'm not sure what time we'll be allowed to use the ballroom that Griffin has organised for us. I was suggesting we go and find something to eat, then I'll check when we can get in the room."

"Great," I answered absently as I looked back at the dark-haired man who was heading to the doorman with a fascinating determination. His face was just so...expressive.

CHAPTER FOUR

Fin

The hotel was the poshest place I'd ever been to, and the dude who stood in front of us in top hat and tails was cool as fuck. I ignored the others because the guy Charlie was talking to was way too sexy, and I had a habit of staring when I didn't intend to.

To keep out of trouble, I lugged the suitcase full of clothes behind me, walking up to the doorman. He didn't so much as bat an eyelid when I stopped in front of him. "What a cool outfit. Did you get to pick it? I mean, you look like you've stepped right out of period drama. I think you'll get a little hot and sticky in the summer. And maybe cold in winter. Do you have a bigger coat you wear?"

His nonplussed face didn't deter me. I pointed at his coat. "Do you have a thicker one for winter?"

A furrow appeared between his brows. "Sir, how can I help you?" he asked, with just the tiniest hint of frustration.

I was used to hearing that tone from others. It was a common occurrence when I forgot myself and asked too many questions at once. "Oh, you want to help me. That's nice. I have a big case. You could lug that for me." I shifted to drag the case in front of me, grinning.

"I'm like seven stone wet through, and these arms aren't really prepared for manual labour, not that I'm lazy. I'm not. It's just that I'm skinny." To make my point, I rolled up the sleeve of my loose-fitting T-shirt and flexed my arm. "See, pitiful."

There was the sound of choked laughter behind me. I glanced back to where Charlie and Guy were standing with Sexy Guy. The guy had really interesting eyes that gleamed like polished onyx. Right now, they were glinting with threads of...well, I wasn't sure, but I sure wished I had a magnifying glass to get a closer look.

"Leave the doorman alone, Fin," Charlie called out. "We'll take the suitcases to the ballroom we're using or, if I can, I'll leave it in the fitting room they'll be allocating us."

"Okay." I glanced back at the dude who hadn't moved and rolled down my sleeve. "What he said. Thanks anyway for the offer to help."

Had he offered?

Did it matter?

Taking hold of the handle, I got no chance to move when Sexy Guy appeared next to me. "I'll carry it for you."

"It's got wheels, so it's more pulling than carrying." I glanced at his arms. "You'll be fine. You seem to have plenty of muscles."

I let go of the handle and gave his bicep a hard squeeze. "Oh yeah, hard and firm. Just what every man wants."

His laughter was bold and free-sounding, mesmerising me. The heat of his skin registered, as did his masculine scent. "You smell as sexy as you look."

"Fuck, he's worse than Nanna," Guy said.

The woman in question came up to me and took hold of my arm. "Come on, Fin, let's go see if the hotel has room service."

"See ya later," I said to Sexy Guy and then let Nanna guide me past the doorman, who looked more than a little bemused.

"Nanna? Nanna, you need to wait for me," Charlie called out. Either Nanna never heard him, or she was in need of a pee because she didn't stop.

At the rate she was pulling me through the reception, I was going with the last option. "I'm sure the reception desk will have a clue to where the bathrooms are," I said, to be helpful.

Nanna patted my arm. "I'm sure they do."

A flushed looking Charlie met us at the large bank of reception desks. The suitcase hit my leg when he stopped. I winced.

"Nanna, I'm warning you—"

"Charlie boy, now you don't need to take that tone with me. You're not too old to go over my knee."

Charlie rolled his eyes and turned to the receptionist, who seemed to be taking a lot of interest in our conversation. "Griffin Hudson has made a booking for the fashion show that's happening tomorrow. People will be arriving through the afternoon, and I sent Luke, the hotel manager, a list of everyone's names as he requested."

"Yes Sir, I have the booking. The manager has decided to give you a full floor of rooms."

"That's cool. A slumber party in a hotel." I aimed a wink at Nanna. "You up for that?"

"Oh son, at my age, I'm up for anything."

It seemed we were setting the trend as I heard more choked laughter. I didn't need to look for the source, though as Sexy Guy was stood not four feet from me.

Was he following us? Was he one of those nosy people?

Charlie distracted me by apologising for Nanna for what felt like the tenth time, though I wasn't sure why. The receptionist worked fast and started the booking process.

"Don't you have an overnight bag?" Nanna questioned as she glanced at my empty hands.

I shoved my hand into a pocket of my baggy jeans and pulled at a small, clear plastic bag that held a fold away toothbrush, a tiny tube of toothpaste and a small tin of deodorant. As I held it out to her, I shoved my other hand into my other pocket and pulled out a rolled-up pair of skimpy pants. "I have."

"You're priceless," Sexy Guy said, laughter lines appearing around his eyes and mouth.

Fuck, he really was sexy.

"I know." I shoved everything back into my pockets, pretending I wasn't getting hot under the collar with all the attention I was getting from him.

"Let's go and check out the rooms. Rachael, what room number is yours?" Nanna asked as she looked at the other woman, who'd been waiting quietly next to Guy.

Rachael held up the old fashioned key and smiled. "1021."

"I hope that's next to me," I said.

The receptionist looked at me. "Sir, your name?"

"No, it's not Sir, it's Fin." I gave her a nice smile so as not to hurt her feelings. "I'm not into kinky stuff, and I'm sorry, but you aren't my type."

There was a muttered curse, which I thought came from Guy, but I wasn't sure because the loud laughter coming from Nanna drowned out everything else.

"Do you have his room key?" Nanna asked the now flushed looking girl.

"Here you go, and it's 1020."

I nodded and held my hand out to Nanna. "It's so cool that they haven't reverted to plastic cards. I'll have to let my mum know that there is one hotel still keen on perseveration." I glanced about and really took in the grand foyer. The details looked original; the cornices and ceiling decorations were possibly eighteenth century. "Is there a book on the history of the hotel?" I asked no one in particular.

"I'll ask Griffin for you," Charlie offered.

"You like history?" Sexy guy questioned, lounging gracefully against the reception desk.

"I hope so. I'm doing a masters in it. Well, not in it, because the past is gone, and all we have are what's been reported in books and at archaeological sites. I mean, it might not all be true, but that's the fun, right? Figuring out if there is a realm of possibility in the supposed facts."

"You're quite right." He didn't sound in the least condescending, which was unusual. Normally by now, when a person met me for the first time, they'd be either running for the hills or giving me a 'is this guy for real' expression. I was used to it, so it didn't bother me. Sexy Guy wasn't doing either of those things, which I made a note to think about when I was alone.

Minutes later, we all got into the lift to head to the floor we needed. The rich scent of Sexy Guy was all I could smell as he stood right next to me. He appeared relaxed as he leant back on the mirrored wall, a bag slung over his shoulder and one in his hand. "Are you a photographer?"

His grin was instant. "Nothing gets past you, does it?"

He didn't sound flippant...but. "All the time, but I eventually catch up." I glanced at Charlie, who was looking at his phone. Finally, my brain figured out why the guy was still with us. "Charlie, is this the guy you were raving about? The one you had a crush on?"

The silence that descended on the lift lasted two seconds before everyone, bar Charlie, who was scowling at me, laughed. Charlie went a beautiful shade of red as Guy covered his mouth and appeared to try and contain his laughter behind his hand. He failed. Nanna, Rachael, and Sexy Guy didn't bother to try to conceal theirs.

"Dude, did you have to blurt that out?" Charlie gave Sexy Guy an apologetic smile. "Sorry, Marcus, you'll get used to Fin and his sudden outbursts. Marcus Crestwell, meet Finlo Denning."

I shrugged my shoulders. "That or you'll run like most people do."

Marcus moved closer and ran a hand down my arm, leaning in close enough I could feel his breath on my cheek. "People can be stupid. I pride myself on trying to avoid that state of being as often as possible."

My heart fluttered in my chest like a trapped bird. I turned my head to look Sexy Guy...Marcus, in the eye. What was there was surprising: desire. I wasn't naive, and I'd had boyfriends in the past. They might not have lasted long because I was a lot to deal with, but I understood attraction. It was certainly not a reaction I was used to, and definitely not one that people displayed very often. It was a pity Marcus was going to get to see me next to naked. That was going to wipe that look right out of his eyes for sure. "It's such a shame you'll see me naked."

"Dude," Guy said in a strangled voice. Nanna, however, lifted her hand for a high five, which I hit without thought. The lift doors opened and saved me from looking at Marcus because this time, I could feel heat creeping up my neck. I really hadn't meant to say that aloud. Me and my no-filter brain would never learn.

In my hotel room a few minutes later, I shut the door and, for good measure, locked it. Resting back against it, I tried to get the image of Marcus's sexy smile out of my head.

"You don't need anyone derailing your last year of uni. You don't." Even saying the words aloud didn't help. I got a sinking feeling that if Marcus decided to set those sexy eyes in my direction, I'd be like a lamb to the slaughter. Not that I ate lamb, it was totally cruel to rear babies then chop them up to give someone a meal. *I mean, really.*

CHAPTER FIVE

Marcus

I couldn't remember the last time I'd had this much fun. The room buzzed with contagious excitement. Agnes, or Nanna as she insisted I call her, and Rachael were hilarious, with a seemingly boundless supply of energy. The dress rehearsal for the fashion show had set off my muse button, which didn't happen often, but a certain someone had more than captured my attention.

Although, Brett, Guy's boyfriend, and Nanna had also held some of my attention too. Griffin had shown up, and for some reason that I couldn't fathom, Nanna had acted like she'd not known who I was. The woman was either a great actress or had the memory of a sieve. It really could be either. What I did know was she was incorrigible and had a lot of ideas on how I should take photos of her and some of the others in the show. I'd listened, to be polite, but in the end, I'd given in and taken some of the shots she'd suggested.

Finlo, on the other hand, had seemed to purposefully avoid me. It seemed he was working hard to fade into the background, and he might have succeeded if Guy hadn't made him an outfit that drew attention to his angular face and disguised how thin he was. The grey-and-black boiler suit was chic, and Guy used some gel to style his hair just right. This allowed me to see all the angles of his face, and I'd not been able to get enough pictures of him. He was just so expressive.

It also hadn't helped when he'd stripped down to the tiniest pair of bright orange pants that hugged his arse to perfection. Was it creepy if I'd taken one or two shots of him wearing nothing but those pants? No, I'm a professional.

A professional perv, a sly, familiar voice suggested.

Buggering to all hell.

I promised myself I'd not develop the film…maybe.

Guy's strained voice pulled me from my thoughts. "Nanna, you need to remember to keep in time to the music. There has to be a twenty-second gap between you and Louise. She has to have time to reach the end of the runway, stop and give two twirls before heading back to you. You should pass about a foot from the end of the runway."

Nanna's hands went to her hips as she eyed Louise, one of the other models I'd met last night. "Can't you walk a bit faster?"

Louise's face was full of laughter. "Agnes, if I go faster, no one will see the gorgeous designs Charlie and Guy have created."

I framed the shot and took several pictures.

"You do know I'm old and have a dodgy hip, right?"

"Agnes, give over," Louise choked out, past gales of laughter.

Agnes stared at Guy and shrugged her shoulders. "I like her."

"Yes, she's great. But we need to figure out a way to get you to slow down."

My phone rang and distracted me. I reached into my jean pocket and checked the number. I stepped away from the end of the stage to answer. "Mom, everything okay?"

"You tell me? I'm sat at a table in The Worthington with Jed. Why are you not here?"

Shit, I'd forgotten I'd set up the meal. The one I'd no intention of attending. I glanced about the noisy room and grinned at the non-lie I was about to tell. "I'm stuck at the dress rehearsal, sorry. I'll foot the bill for you and Jed—"

"Marcus—"

"Gotta go. I'll see you tomorrow." I clicked off the phone and turned it to silent the second it started to ring again, shoving it into my rear pocket with a grin attached to my face.

"Did you do something naughty? You have a look on your face that says you did," Finlo asked quietly.

I glanced sideways, eyes widening. "You've good stealth skills," I said, avoiding his question.

He nodded. "I do. When you're a little weird, you need them."

My stomach twisted into a tight ball at his answer. His face showed no distress, but I got the impression he'd been given a hard time more than once in his life.

"You get picked on at school?" I found myself asking. I hated personal questions, so I was prepared for him to tell me where to get off.

"Some, but I wasn't there long enough for the kids to get into their stride." He shrugged.

I leant against the wall and stared at him. "Didn't you go to school?"

"Mum taught me at home. She doesn't like pigeons to be put into a box. It was easier after that. I've a flexible mind, only it can flex a little too fast for conservative methods of teaching."

The guy had a way of speaking that could make him sound dumb and like the cleverest person in the room. He was fascinating. I nodded. "Many schools only focus on those who fit into what society deems as normal," I sighed.

My best friend Colin hadn't fit into any box either and had struggled for years until he'd started to paint. Now, the guy was so sought after, he couldn't keep up with the number of commissions he had for his artwork. The teachers in the private school had all said he'd amount to nothing, but they were wrong.

"Did they do that to you?" His brow rumpled in a way that made me want to run my thumb over it to smooth it out.

I held on to my camera a little tighter. "Not me, my best friend Colin. Teachers are all about academia and not about the creative personality." Seeing I was about to start to lecture on the topic, I waved my camera at him. "I should get back to work."

"See ya," he said, spinning around and leaving me staring at his retreating back.

I chuckled. My early thoughts about whether I was ready to date came back to me. My smile widened. Finlo was clearly a literal thinking guy, which was something I'd need to remember because dating looked to be back on the agenda.

The dress rehearsal the day before had gone without too many disasters, I wasn't sure what this evening would bring, but there were a few worried faces. Nanna marching over to Guy and a pasty looking Brett captured my attention. Brett looked terrified as she took hold of his hand. "Come with me. Don't worry, Guy, he'll be fine."

I followed them, taking a picture of Agnes as she smiled at Brett, but then she shifted and turned her back on the room. What was she up to?

Unable to resist seeing what the mischief-maker was up to, I walked around the edge of the room that was being used as a changing area.

At her words, "take a good nip," I shook my head. I glanced in Guy's direction to see if he was watching.

When Brett coughed and spluttered out, "Holy mother…what…is that?" I looked back to see his face was flushed, and his eyes were watering.

"Don't you be worrying your pretty little head about what it is. Let's just say it's premium stuff."

"Premium? I think it's just removed my stomach lining and killed a few million brain cells." Brett licked at his lips, his eyes looking a little unfocused. "Shit, how can that already be having an effect?"

"I told you, it's premium stuff. Here, have another swig."

The temptation to step in and stop her was outweighed by how relaxed Brett became. Leaving them to it, I went back to taking shots of the chaos in the room.

"We've got fifteen minutes to show time. Time to get changed, guys," Guy shouted.

Taking that as my cue to head back into the main ballroom, I turned and saw Finlo staring at himself in the mirror. The day before, I'd got a few shots of him dressed as he was now, yet there was something different this time. A confidence in his posture that hadn't been there the day before. I took several shots before I even realised I'd lifted my camera.

Beautiful.

His gaze met mine in the mirror, and his lips lifted into a smile that lit his face. A warmth spread through the centre of my body. I wasn't sure how long we stood just staring at each other, but when I turned away, I understood that in those moments, something had changed between us. I wanted more than just simple fucking, that was for sure. How much more, though, was a question I couldn't answer.

A little breathless, I went out past the curtain and took a deep, shaky breath, then another. My hand was slippery on the leather strap of my camera. Get it together!

"There you are. I'm starting to think you're avoiding me."

My mum stood next to Jed, her face not giving her away, although palpable frustration came off her body in waves. "I'm working, Mum. How can I be avoiding you?"

Narrowing the small distance between us, I bent and brushed a kiss over her cheek. "And you had a more than willing man to keep you company," I said, quietly enough that no one else would hear.

"Are you playing matchmaker?" she hissed out, maybe a little louder than me but not loud enough for Jed to hear.

The lights flashed to indicate the show was about to start. "Go and watch the show. I'll see you later."

She gave me a look I recognised. It said that she wasn't going to let the subject drop. That was okay because I wasn't going to either. It was time she started to live a little, and that applied to me too.

A quiet fell over the ballroom as the room turned to black, then Guy's voice announced the beginning of the show. Thoughts of my mother were forgotten when lights illuminated the runway and music started to play. I captured the empty stage, then each model as they appeared. Guided then by the play of light, the outfits, and the expressions of those in the crowded seats.

Without thought, I moved closer to the stage, recalling when Finlo was due to appear. Crouching at the end of the runway, Finlo appeared, his gaze on some unknown point. He walked with measured steps, and it was all I could do to remember to press the shutter on my camera.

Fuck a duck!

CHAPTER SIX

Finlo

L istening to the lecturer, I wrote several notes in the margin of the book I'd bought from the charity shop. It had been a real find. The original cost was ninety pounds, and I'd got this copy for a pound. Mum hadn't been overly keen on me coming to uni, but I'd seen it as an adventure. The tests they'd made me sit to assess my academic ability had been awful. I wasn't sure I'd pass, not because I couldn't answer the questions, but because it only took me half the time of everyone else. I had a tendency to run rather than walk, which suited my brain, but sometimes I could miss the important stuff, which isn't a good thing in exams.

"Mr. Denning, can you explain what is so fascinating out the window?" Mr. Thornhill's tone held a wealth of exasperation.

Crap. Sure enough, I was gazing out the window. I shrugged. "Nothing that I can see," I answered honestly.

"Then do you think you could keep your focus here," Mr. Thornhill requested.

"Like he can do that," someone muttered just loud enough for me to hear, accompanied by several titters of laughter.

I didn't bother to look at the room. "I'll do my best," I offered because what else could I do. Mum had said it was all anyone could do, and I aimed for that as much as possible.

Mr. Thornhill was an okay lecturer, but he could be a bit boring and dry. I'd pointed out in my very first lecturer that if he spiced things up that maybe people wouldn't be distracted by things going on around them. He'd not listened. The stuff he shared was about as dry as a piece of cardboard.

There was a nudge to my elbow, and I glanced at Pippa. "You're doing it again," she whispered.

I glanced about, my brow raising. "Doing what?"

She giggled and shook her head. "Looking out the window, you dork."

There was only humour in her voice and no insult. She was possibly the only real friend I had at uni. She was also a history major, with plans to work as a teacher in the future. She had her life mapped out. I liked that about her. I sometimes daydreamed it would be nice to be a little more Pippa than me.

"You've gone again," she hissed, right before there was a frustrated sounding sigh coming from the front of the class.

Twisting in my seat, so my back was to the window, I made a show of purposefully looking at the front of the room.

That had to help?

An hour later, I wasn't sure if Mr. Thornhill would require medical attention; his face was so red. I'd kept my focus, but that hadn't helped because then I'd a few questions I wanted answered. As we exited the room, Pippa slipped her arm through mine. Her ponytail bobbed and brushed at my shoulder as she walked with me. She was only a couple of inches shorter than me and had curves that many guys took notice of.

"Mr. Thornhill is never gonna forgive you for that first day, is he?"

I sighed regretfully. "No. It's been nearly four years."

She rubbed at the arm she was holding with her other hand. "Not long now, and we'll be free to venture out into the big world." The enthusiasm was something else I liked about Pippa.

"You know what you want to do. Me, I'm still waiting to be inspired."

I was tugged out of the building into the brightness of the afternoon. The sun was high in the bold blue sky, and I stopped, shutting my eyes while I tilted my head back to enjoy the warmth bathing my skin.

A bag knocked my elbow, and my eyelids fluttered open to watch several people rush past us. "Why doesn't anyone stop and appreciate the moment?"

Pippa laughed loudly. "You stop and appreciate it for everyone." She tugged at me. "Come on, let's go to Billie's for a smoothie. I haven't had a chance to ask about the fashion show."

Onyx eyes that I'd had more than one dream about formed in my mind, and a smile spread over my face. "Marcus Crestwell, have you heard of him?" Other than Charlie raving about him, I'd never heard of him before the fashion show. I'd righted that, only to find myself a little obsessed with his work.

"I've got one of his books."

I stopped walking. "You have?"

"I do. And why do you sound so shocked? Think about it, Fin. He travels to places where history is being made and captures it for future generations to look back on, like us now."

"Wow, I like the way you look at that." I scratched at my jaw, then realised I'd forgotten to shave again. "Can I see your book?"

A wrinkle appeared between her brows. "I think I have it here. If not, I'll ask Mun to send it to me for you if you want?"

"Yeah. I don't have the cash to buy any more books right now." I was on a very tight budget. With Mum disagreeing with me being here, she'd been resistant to helping pay, but I'd managed to get a grant, and I'd a part-time job in Billie's smoothie bar. Billie was a friend of Mum's, so she understood my eccentricities and didn't mind if I went off on a tangent.

"Wanna go see if I've got it now?" Pippa was a generous soul.

"Please. He's gorgeous and gay. Did you know that? It's his eyes that draw me though. I could get lost in them. There was a moment when they met mine in the mirror, and I felt something deep inside me. He's a very interesting man."

Pippa stared at me open-mouthed.

"Are you trying to catch flies or something?"

"You like him?"

"Isn't that what I just said?" I ran over what I'd said. Yeah, I'd made that clear. I touched a hand to her forehead to see if she had a fever. "You feeling all right?"

"I'm fine," she said, shaking off my hand, "it's just that you've never said you liked a boy before."

"I'm gay. Why wouldn't I like a boy? Did you think I liked you in that way? I'm sorry if I led you on. That was never my intention."

Laughter lines appeared around her eyes and mouth. "God, I love you."

Heat suffused my face, and my pulse kicked up a bit of a stink. "Oh, now see, this is not good. I'm sorry, but I can't make my cock like you. It's just something I'll never be able to do. It knows what it wants."

Her body shuddered, laughter peeling out of her. "Oh sweet Jesus…you're…the best…friend ever."

I released a breath and nodded. "Yes, friends. Not the kind with benefits," I pointed out, just to be clear.

"Friends. I get it." Her eyes twinkled. "Let's go and see if I have the book. Then you can tell me all about Marcus."

"And Nanna."

"Nanna? Whose Nanna? I didn't think you had any other relatives aside from your mum?"

I grinned at her confused expression. "I don't. Nanna belongs to Charlie, and she adopted me. She has this amazing talking cat, Cissy."

"Oh right. You do know how to find—"
"Good friends?"
The laughter returned. "Yeah, let's go with that. Now come on."

The room I had off-campus was nothing more than a shoebox, but it was what I could afford. I flopped down on the single bed and stared at the ceiling, feeling a little... I wasn't quite sure what I was feeling. Pippa had pointed out more than once how much I liked Marcus, and thankfully she'd dropped the subject of loving me. She'd found the book on her bookshelf, and it was now in my bookbag. The temptation to look at it again was there.

The few hours I'd spent in Pippa's room talking and looking at the pictures left an impression on my soul. I'd found myself entranced by images that transported me right into the moment Marcus had captured them. The man had serious skills, that was for sure. It was there, in the depth of the emotion the picture conveyed.

Did it hurt him to take such pictures?

I suspected it did. There was too much feeling in them for it not to hurt.

The man had given me his number after the fashion show, suggesting I give him a call if I wanted to see him again. I rolled onto my side to reach for the piece of paper I'd kept, even after I'd put the number into my phone.

It wasn't often that I thought about an action before doing it. That I'd set the paper aside meant something, although I wasn't sure what. I ran my fingers over the soft square.

The guy had struck me as a player. I was good at reading people. Yet his pictures spoke of more depth than he portrayed on first impressions.

I slipped my hand into my pocket and pulled out my phone.

It's Fin.

Send.

CHAPTER SEVEN

Marcus

In the past week, I'd heard nothing from Fin, and I'd found myself doubting the moment of connection. I'd sulked a little when I'd had a few minutes down time to think about it. Or when Steve had pointed it out while he'd laughed at me. I'd made the first move. It was up to him now.

Wasn't it?

Fuck, I was acting...*stupid*.

The vibration in my back pocket was ignored for the moment as I swished a sheet of paper in some developing fluid, the image coming to life before my eyes.

I'd lasted six days, five hours and fourteen minutes before I'd given in and come down to my dark room. The reel of film I'd left only part developed had all but called my name. It was a tricky one.

How tricky was it, really?

The image of Finlo appeared in the red light. Long, lithe lines, sharp angles, and a butt you could eat a meal off. The heavens had blessed him for sure. A little hot under the collar, I tried to look at the photos I'd taken objectively. Light, angle, shade, composition.

I cursed long and loud. All my eyes could focus on was Finlo.

Jerking at the knock to the door behind me, I glanced around furtively before I realised Steve wouldn't walk in when I was working.

"I'm off. I've sent the stills to Sigrid and Griffin that you picked for the campaign. Don't forget I'll be in late tomorrow."

I had forgotten. Shit, did I have anything that needed doing? After a few seconds, there was a louder knock.

"Answer me, you fucker."

"Nice," I shout back. "Go on and enjoy your time off."

"Yeah, will do." Silence followed, and I waited a couple of minutes before I went back to what I was doing, feeling inexplicably guilty.

My pocket vibrated again, reminding me I'd not looked at the first message I'd got. I placed down the tongs I was using and reached for my phone, squinting in the eerie, glowing light of my darkroom.

Unable to make out the names, I laid my phone down and checked the images were fully developed before I went to switch on the light. Picking my phone back up, a smile spread over my face at seeing the message from my mother.

You owe me an explanation.

I'd managed to avoid her since the fashion show, but Jed had messaged to say she was on the warpath. The thank-you he'd also given me made me wonder if things had worked the way I'd wanted them to.

No clue what you're talking about.

I typed quickly, grinning as I hit send.

The next message was short and to the point.

It's Fin

What did that even mean? I scratched at the side of my head, my gaze going to the pictures that I'd developed days ago of the catwalk show. I'd way more of Finlo than anyone else. Well, maybe Nanna and Brett equalled him. Brett because he'd got a little too tipsy on whatever was in Nanna's hip flash. The guy had worked the runway like a pro until he'd lost his footing at the end of the catwalk and toppled into the lap of several people. I'd managed to capture the moment, which I'd only be sharing with Guy and Brett. They were decent men, and it would be up to them to decide what they did with the pictures I'd taken for fun.

I hesitated for a few more seconds, trying to get into Finlo's head. I gave up and hit dial after saving his number into my phone.

"Hello?"

"Hey, it's Marcus."

"Yes, it says so on my screen."

I chuckled. "You messaged."

"I did."

My laughter increased. "Would you like to go out for a drink? Maybe something to eat?"

"When? Now?"

"Now might be a bit tricky as I'm in London, and I assume you're in Brighton?"

"That's a silly thing to assume when I told you I live in Brighton."

His answer was a total Finlo thing to say. The hours I'd spent with him had given me a little insight into his thought patterns, or lack thereof. "It was, and you're right." I checked my wristwatch. It was too late to travel down to Brighton tonight. "It's a little late to come tonight. What about tomorrow...oh fuck, tomorrow I have a shoot planned for the evening."

"Okay, that would work."

"Pardon?"

"The shoot. Give me the address and the time I need to be there. I'll meet you there."

Was he serious?

"You want to watch me work?"

"It's a date. What we do doesn't matter, does it?"

I rubbed at the side of my jaw, grinning stupidly at the pictures in front of me. "No, I don't suppose it does."

"Great. Send me the information, that way I won't forget it. Bye."

I stared at the phone when it registered he did actually mean 'bye'. The smile remained glued to my lips as I sent him a message with all the details for the next day. The guy was...I wasn't sure, but the excitement buzzing through me was something I could get used to.

I wasn't at all sure what to expect the next day as I stood outside the chic looking shop waiting for Finlo to arrive. I clutched at the strap of my camera bag, scanning the crowded street for Fin. It took a few seconds to notice him as he strolled through the throngs of people down Carnaby Street.

He fitted right in dressed in what had to be recycled clothing, none of which fit him. The dungarees hid most of the T-shirt that had possibly once been bright and colourful but now looked like it had seen one too many washes. The denim jacket hanging off one shoulder had an eclectic mix of badges someone had lovingly sewn on by hand if the stitching was anything to go by. He wore Doc Martin's that were black with a red rose pattern over them.

Since I'd last seen him, it looked like someone had cut his hair with a pair of pinking shears. It was stuck up at odd angles that highlighted his slashing cheekbones.

His mouth was a little too wide, which was more noticeable when he grinned at me and picked up his pace. "I'm not late," he said the second he came to a halt in front of me.

"I didn't think you would be."

The smile got bigger, if it was at all possible, and looked to be reaching for his ears. "I'm good with time keeping, mostly. But when it's important, like now when you've got to work, I made an effort to get here so as not to piss off your boss."

I chuckled. "No one's the boss of me, Fin." I nodded to the shop door. "Shall we go in?"

"Why are you asking me?"

"No clue," I answered, trying to contain my laughter. I opened the door to let him pass. There was a momentary look of confusion before he stepped into the shop.

He stopped when Simone appeared from the back room. She was an intimidating sight at six-foot, with striking blue hair and contact lenses that made her eyes look a cat's.

"Simone, this is Finlo—"

"I prefer Fin. My mum is the only one who calls me Finlo, and it's normally when she's frustrated with me."

Simone held out her hand, the light catching the many rings she wore. Her face had a polite smile on it as her eyes met mine over Fin's head. "Fin it is. Are you here to help Marcus?"

It was a valid question, and I held my breath to see what Fin's answer would be.

"It's a date. I've spent a few hours looking over Marcus's use of light in the composition of his pictures. I'm not sure I'd be expert enough to comment on how to change things up to make them better. He already has an amazing ability to frame a subject to make them the focus of the image. I'd say you're in good hands with him."

His utter seriousness left me a little stunned. Not about the date—I'd kind of expected that—but his comment about my work.

"A date, really?" Simone asked, breaking my concentration.

"Yes." Fin frowned and glanced from Simone to me. "That's right?"

I nodded. "Fin is going to get his first lesson in photography."

He clapped his hands together. "I knew this was going to be a great date."

Simone gave us both an odd look before she indicated to the door she'd come out of. "Shall we get started?"

"Let's," Fin answered, beaming at us both.

CHAPTER EIGHT

Finlo

When Marcus had said he was going to give me a lesson in photography, I'd been a little dubious. I had no skills when it came to gadgets of any kind, and I tended to break things, so I'd learnt to avoid anything that required a degree in technology.

"Fin, if you stand over there by the wall, I want you to look at the model and tell me what you see."

I could do that. Maybe.

The two models, one male and one female, were perfect. Their skin was flawless under the lights that Marcus had positioned next to a black velvet high back chair. There was a coat in a bold lime placed over the high wing of the seat. The guy was dressed head to toe in black, whereas the woman wore all white. The coat was the feature, or that's what I imagined because it was where my gaze went.

"The choice of chair and the outfits allow for the coat hanging on the seat to become the focus. The models are superfluous. Is that the point?"

Simone laughed, whereas both models wore matching pinched expressions that Marcus captured, making me grin. "I bet that'll be a great photo."

The wicked grin, one I was getting used to seeing on Marcus's face, appeared as he winked at me. "You're right about the focus of the shot, but the models will give contrast to the image and help focus the eye where we want it."

He continued to explain what he was doing as he moved around the small room out the back of the shop we were using. For a time, the only sound in the room came from the camera's shutter as Marcus took what felt like hundreds of shots. He checked the camera's tiny screen several times, offering it up for me to look at the image. I wasn't exactly sure what I was supposed to be looking at, but he seemed pleased if I made a comment about what I could see.

Several outfits and I was sure a thousand pictures later, we were out on the street. "That was great. What happens next?"

"I'll develop the images and pick the ones I think will work with the brief that Simone gave me." He slung the camera bag over his shoulder, then he held out his hand towards me, wiggling his fingers.

I eyed his hand. "You want to hold my hand?" I checked because I didn't always pick up the right signals, even when they were obvious, like now.

In answer, he took hold of my hand. "What time is your train back to Brighton?"

"Oh, I'm not going back tonight."

"You're not?"

"No."

He stared at me, a furrow appearing between his brows. "Are you planning on spending the night… at mine?" There wasn't so much as a flicker of emotion.

I tilted my head, trying to figure out if I'd picked up the wrong signals. "Isn't that what you want? Most dates I've gone on, not that I've had many, but those I have had..." I rubbed at my temples.

"Erm, maybe I shouldn't be talking about past dates. I mean, it's not like any of them were as attractive as you, but it's a little rude to talk about sex with other people on a first date, even if there is an expectation of getting naked."

I looked up sheepishly and saw Marcus rubbing his eyes with his free hand.

"Have I fucked up? I've fucked up. I'll just go home." I shrugged and decided I didn't like the feeling of disappointment that followed, which was strange because I was never normally bothered one way or another.

His fingers clasped mine tighter. "Let's go grab something to eat. I'm starved. We can talk about the rest later."

Letting him lead seemed like the right thing to do, so we ambled down the still busy street, no one paying us any attention. We stopped outside a place that looked way posher than somewhere I could afford on my tight budget. "This looks like it has tables free."

"Can we check the prices first? I'm on a budget."

"You're my date, right?"

Was this a trick question? "Yes."

"Then I'll be paying." Marcus seemed to think that was the end of the discussion, opening the door with his free hand and tugged me in behind him.

"You want to Dutch?" I persisted. I'd been out before and ended up forking out more cash than I could afford, then had to live off cheese on toast for two weeks. It had put me right off cheese for several months. I like cheese and would prefer to keep on liking it.

The smile was back. "I'll be paying, but if it makes you feel awkward, when we have our next date, you can buy the meal."

"There's going to be another date? You know this already, but you haven't seen me naked."

The waiter who'd come to seat us stopped so suddenly, the couple walking behind him had to jerk to the side to avoid a collision.

Marcus roared with laughter. The waiter continued to stand there, looking uncertain as the couple made a rude comment as they walked past us and out the door. People were so weird sometimes. I rolled my eyes while Marcus took a few seconds to get himself back under control. His eyes were full of mirth as he asked the waiter if they had a table for two. Funny thing was, I got the distinct impression he wasn't laughing at me, but more at the couple's reaction.

A few minutes later, we were sat in a secluded corner. "Were you laughing at the couple?"

His nod was immediate. "People, for whatever reason, don't like blunt honesty. Me, I love that about you."

The blush that followed warmed my skin so much, I had to remove my jacket. I glanced about to distract from the strange undercurrent that was happening between us. The place had lots of dark furniture that wasn't to my taste. The mood lighting cast a cream glow over the table with a couple of candles flickering in the middle. Sniffing the rich, fragrant air, I glanced at those around us to see what the food looked like.

"There's an awful lot of meat on those plates."

Marcus, who'd picked up the menu, lowered it to look at me. "Are you vegetarian? Vegan?"

"I do eat some red meat. Vitamin B12 is essential in the replication of our DNA, and I want to be healthy. The liver can store vitamins for up to seven years, so I calculate eating meat once a year is helpful."

Marcus's elbows were on the table, and he'd cupped his chin. "Is that so?"

"Yep. As I said, my mother home schooled me for ten years. I learnt a lot about the body and what helps to keep it healthy." I leant in a little closer. "Refined sugar is the devil...but I love it." I sighed dejectedly.

The laughter that I was starting to love the sound of poured out of Marcus. "It's good to know that I'm not going to have to try to eat healthily."

"Oh, I'm not one of those people who preach about what others should eat. We all have the facts at our fingertips. It's all about choice. My mother ensured I understood what the downside was to eating too many sugary things, but she left the decision to me about whether I ate them or not."

"She sounds like an interesting lady."

"She is. But when you meet her, you need to remember that whatever topic you first pick to talk about, that's all you'll get to talk about. She likes a good debate." Marcus's brows rose in that way that indicated I might have said something he was surprised by. I went back over what I'd talked about. I shrugged, not able to see what the issue was.

"Where does your mum live?"

I waved a hand. "London. Have you heard of the Elise eco crusader?"

His lips twitched. "Yes...is that your mum?"

"It is."

The waiter that had shown us to the table reappeared. "Are you ready to order?"

"No." I picked up the menu, once again enjoying the sound of Marcus's laughter.

"Can you give us a couple more minutes?"

I was right about the prices. They were extortionate. "Are you sure you can afford this?"

A deep line appeared between his brows. "You're serious, aren't you?"

"About what?" I asked in confusion.

He reached out and laid a hand over mine. "You don't need to worry about whether I can afford the meal. I'm...loaded."

His face got a little pink, but that could have been the mood lighting. "Loaded? As in rich? How much do photographers make? It doesn't seem like a lucrative job. Not if you take into account the cost of travelling and then staying in foreign hotels. Not that I've ever travelled. I'm hoping to one day, but not yet. Uni fees are crippling, and the debt will be with me for...well, I don't know because I've no clue what I'll do once I'm finished."

"In answer to your first question, yes, I've got a lot of money. I make quite a lot from my photography now. In the beginning, I couldn't be choosy about which photoshoots I did." He shrugged. "Now I can pretty much pick and choose what I do."

The menu was forgotten. "How do you choose?"

The smile was appreciative as it widened at me. "Good question. I work with a few people I like, that's important to me as I can be difficult when I work."

"Difficult how? You weren't difficult tonight. Firm, yes, but you were clear and concise. How would that make you difficult?"

"I love you," he said through his laughter.

There were those words again and a warmth I wasn't used to sitting dead centre in my chest. For a moment, I was left speechless. He didn't mean it. Did he? No, it's a joke? But why would someone joke about that?

"Are we ready to order?" The same waiter asked, his face full of expectation as he stood poised with an electronic handheld gadget.

"No."

There was a loud, put-upon sigh that got a brow raise from Marcus. "Do you want a drink? I'll have an espresso martini, please."

The please sounded forced, and Marcus's teeth appeared to be gritted together. "Oh, coffee at this time of the night is bad for me. I'll take…erm," I looked at the list of drinks that mainly consisted of cocktails, "the gin sling, please."

When the guy disappeared, I picked the menu back up, but what Marcus had said nagged like a toothache, and I couldn't concentrate. Knowing I wasn't going to be able to pick food, I glanced back at him. "Why did you say you loved me? It's too soon to make declarations of that kind. Not that I disbelieve that there is such a thing as love at first sight because I do. What I felt when we met was an attraction. Yes, it was stronger than anything I've felt before, but does that mean it's love? You've a beautifully expressive face until you slip that mask on that you wear when I think you're trying to figure stuff out. You're doing it now," I pointed out as his head tilted and his fringe moved over his forehead. Dark eyes glowed, and the warmth continued to linger inside my chest. "Anyway, I like you. I'll be honest that if you're attracted to me, then you might be very disappointed later when I take off my clothes, so be warned."

There was a strangled noise, and I sighed at the waiter, who was standing beside me, holding our drinks. His face was a wonderful shade of ripe tomato. I glanced at the menu and picked the first vegetarian meal on it. "I'll have the vegetable risotto with a side of bruschetta."

Lifting the menu, I held it out and offered a smile of apology. The poor guy evidently had a problem with listening to people's conversations. It did beg the question of why he would work in a place where people were guaranteed to talk.

Marcus ordered a fish dish and waited for the guy to leave before he picked up his drink and took a sip. His gaze held mine, and it felt...intimate. "I forgot how literal you are, Fin. When I said I love you, it was meant in the context of you are a great guy that makes me happy, not the romantic sense."

"Okay." Once more, there was a sliver of disappointment inside me that I'd need to think about later.

He directed the conversation and the meal passed very quickly. Back outside the restaurant, night had fallen, and there was a hard bite to the air. I huddled in my clothes, wishing I'd brought a warmer jacket with me. Marcus slipped the leather one he'd brought around my shoulders, and the scent of his aftershave enveloped me. I sniffed at the collar, enjoying the fragrance.

"Are you sniffing my jacket?"

"Smells so good," I groaned, taking another deep inhale.

His arm slung around my shoulder, and he tugged me closer to his body. "I'm feeling a little jealous of my jacket right now."

I laughed, looking up at him. "It's an inanimate object. Why would you be jealous of it?"

CHAPTER NINE

Marcus

S teve gave me a look that got me out of my seat and heading to the small kitchen I'd had put in when the lower level of the house had been converted. "Do you want a cup of tea?"

"Yeah. But don't drown it with milk," he said.

I glanced back at the man lounging on the leather two-seater. "I don't drown it in milk. You're not a normal person and only tease the tea by showing it the milk then taking it away after feeding it a minuscule drop."

"That's all it bloody needs," he argued back.

Kettle on, I leant against the counter and waited for the other man out. I'd known him too long and knew the questions about my date with Fin were coming.

"How was Simone?"

I rolled my eyes. "You do know how predictable you are?"

He sat forward, shaking his head. "I'm anything but that."

"If you say so. Simone is fine. The hair is currently blue, making her look like a giant smurf."

He coughed. "No way, blue? It was bright orange the last time I saw her. Did you get a picture of her?"

"I wasn't there to take pictures of her."

"That hasn't stopped you in the past," he muttered, just loud enough to be heard over the bubbling kettle.

"I'm a professional," I argued back.

"Professional, pfft. You're a photographer with no understanding of levels of privacy when you want to take a picture." His eyes narrowed on my darkroom door. "I bet you've got hundreds of pictures in there of your new muse."

My brows shot up. "New muse?"

"Yes, new muse. Finlo. How was last night?"

I pointed at him. "See predictable and nosy to boot." Swinging around, I made the tea for

92

us both. Back on the sofa, I sat opposite him and sipped at my hot tea.

It took four minutes and eleven seconds before Steve caved. "All right, I'm predictable, but you've not been on a date in...well, I can't remember the last time. I'm your friend. I want to see you happy, and since you met this guy, you've not stopped talking about him."

"Untrue." I hadn't, had I? I shook off the oddness of that notion. I'd never talked a lot about any of the guys I'd dated in the past. And Fin and I were dating, after the awkwardness of him announcing he was coming back for sex, the evening had been fun. He'd not seemed disappointed when I'd organised and paid for an uber to take him all the way back to Brighton as he'd missed the last train. As much as I'd wanted to get him naked, the way other men had treated him left me wanting to show him there were decent men out there. I'd not wanted him to feel...I wasn't sure what he felt. It was hard to judge. He was so literal sometimes, it took me a few beats to catch up with him.

That he'd not argued with me sending him home was...good...bad? The peck on the lips I'd initiated had fallen a little flat. Had it been more like a brotherly kiss?

"Why are you frowning?"

I glanced over the rim of my mug. "If you expect to go back to a guy's for sex, and that guy sends you home, would you be disappointed?"

It was Steve's turn to frown. "Is that what happened? Was he expecting sex?"

Another sip of tea didn't help me figure out how to answer that one. "He's a literal thinker. I think he applies what he's learnt about his dating experience to what he thinks will happen."

"Interesting, so guys he's dated in the past were just after sex. Has he had a long term relationship?"

"Not from what he mentioned." I chuckled, recalling how he'd go off on a tangent that left me rushing to catch up. I'd been left with the impression that he had a few hang-ups about his body, and that came from men once they'd seen him naked. He'd mentioned it more than once through the night like he was warning me off. He'd not registered that I'd seen him in tiny underwear that had left little to the imagination. He was slim and all angles. His body was beautiful, and if I were honest—and I always was with myself—I'd more than once pleasured myself to the thought of getting my hands and mouth on Fin's body.

"Didn't he show the right level of disappointment when you sent him on his merry way?"

I drained the last of the tea and placed the mug down on the small table between us. "He's expressive in so many ways. Then he's like a closed book," I said, running my hands through my hair. "He's…fascinating."

Steve's lips twitched. "You sound smitten."

Smitten, was that what I was?

"Get a grip. Smitten? What kind of word is that?" One that, when I considered it, seemed to fit the situation and these strange feelings for Fin, not that I'd admit that to Steve.

"It's a great word. It means to be strongly attracted to someone or something. There are a load of synonyms such as fond of, taken with, attracted to, charmed by, captivated by, enchanted by, in love with. I could go on."

A flutter started in the base of my stomach at the last one. "You've watched too much Countdown. You think you're in dictionary corner," I said, hoping to change the topic. No one needed to be mentioning the L word.

He beamed at me before standing and picking up my dirty mug, heading to the kitchen. "I'm taking that as a compliment."

"You would," I fired back, grinning.

There was the sound of running water and clinking before Steve came back and remained standing. "When will I get to meet Finlo? You could bring him to the party on Saturday?"

I forced my smile to remain in place. Steve was hosting a party for his boyfriend, and I'd no way of getting out of it. Spending any length of time with Steve's boyfriend meant I'd go home with aching teeth from how often I'd have to clamp them together to keep from saying something that would only piss Steve off. Fin would be a great distraction. The idea of seeing him gave me a boost almost as good as a caffeine fix. "That's a great idea. I'll ring him later and ask if he's free."

"I'm sure he'll be free for you."

"That's what I like, confidence in my abilities."

He scowled. "You don't need any more of that! Now should we get back to work?"

I got up and clapped him on the shoulder. "You've a short memory. You were the one who wanted to take a break so you could be nosy."

"Concerned, not nosy. There's a difference."

He strolled back across the room to his office desk. "If you say so," I muttered at his back.

I'd waited until Steve had finally left for the day before I went up to retrieve my personal mobile. I'd learnt very early on that using your personal phone for work meant someone was always trying to get in touch at the most inopportune moments. As a result, I had a work mobile that I carried about in the daytime. My personal one tended to live in my camera bag or was left upstairs when I was working down in the darkroom. It drove my mother nuts as I didn't always get to answer her immediately.

Several minutes later, I cursed as I dialled my personal mobile, hoping I'd not switched it to silent. The only drawback with two mobiles was that I often misplaced one of them, like now. The distant sound of my ringtone left me heading up to my bedroom. There, on the bedside cabinet built into the massive bed frame, was my phone. Turning off my work phone, I put that down to retrieve the other one, then started to curse again.

Thanks for last night. It was fun.

You've not replied, so I'm taking that as you're not interested.

Or I could be wrong, and you're busy. If that's the case, ignore the second message.

Or maybe not and ignore the message before this one.

There was an hour between each message, and the last one had been ten minutes earlier. I hit dial and prayed he'd answer.

"Hello."

My heart sank at the hesitancy in his voice. "Hey Fin, last night was fun, and yes, I'm interested," I rushed in first. I took a breath to steady the nerves prancing about inside me. "Sorry for not answering sooner. It's just I leave my personal phone in the house when

I'm working." I rolled my eyes to the ceiling at my own lameness. I sat on the edge of the bed, my palms feeling way sweatier than they should be.

"I see."

Silence followed, and I pulled the phone from my ear to glance at the screen. Putting it back. "You still there?"

"Of course."

I chuckled, my mood lifting. "I'm ringing to see if you fancy coming to a party with me on Saturday."

"Another date...to a party? Erm, what kind of party is it? Will I be expected to dress up because I don't have anything that fits for a super posh event? Although shabby chic is a thing right now, isn't it? Could I carry off shabby chic?"

The grin on my face made it ache. It was so wide. "The kind with food, drink and scintillating company...that's me, by the way. Dress code is whatever you feel comfortable in."

That got a laugh, and I grinned.

"Okay."

"Okay, as in yes, you'll come with me?"

"Isn't that what I said?"

The confusion was adorable. "My mistake, you did. If you give me your address, I'll drive down to Brighton and pick you up. And if you like, you could plan to stay over."

There was a kind of breathy noise. "So, to be clear, we'll be getting naked this time?"

"That's optional as I have a spare room you can use if you want it." I sucked in a fortifying breath. "Listen, Fin, I don't know what your dates consisted of in the past, but I'm a more go with the flow and see how we both feel in the moment, kinda guy. Is that all right?" I held my breath and waited.

"The moment yesterday wasn't the right one, is that what you're saying? But you think there'll be other moments that are right...for us?"

"Yes, I do." Before I could explain further, he spoke.

"How will you know when those moments are? I've not always been great at picking up signals, and this has... see, I'm about to start talking about other men. Pippa says that talking about exes goes down like a lead balloon. Not that a balloon full of lead would be up in the air to start with."

His genuine concern tugged the smile off my lips. Guys could be real dicks. "It's fine. How about I tell you when I'm making a move on you?"

There was a long, drawn-out sigh that was worrying until he answered, "That sounds like a good plan."

"Great. Now relax about the naked part. Text me your address and what time works best for you for me to pick you up."

I was already shifting through my mind what I'd originally planned for Saturday to make sure I'd be able to go and get Fin. With the details confirmed, he hardly gave me time to say goodbye before I could hear the dial tone. Laughing, I got up and dropped my phone on the bed. The guy had an innate ability to make me...*happy*. I stopped when my heart kicked up a little bit of a fuss at just *how happy* he made me.

Too soon.

Was it?

It was way too soon for feels.

CHAPTER TEN

Finlo

Nanna was a wise woman, so I headed to her home on Friday evening. Or was it classed as Charlie and Griffin's home? Did it matter?

I pondered that all the way to the house. I'd rung Nanna earlier to check she wasn't going out, and she'd seemed only too happy for me to pay her a visit. I clearly hadn't put her off with my visits before the fashion show, which was a good thing. It also appeared I'd not put Marcus off either.

It was a funny position, not funny ha ha, but funny strange. For the first time that I could remember, I cared about what someone thought about me. I'd brought over some of the clothes I had picked out for Saturday's date, and I was hoping Nanna could help me decide. This was a whole new concept for me. I'd never really been bothered before by what anyone thought of my clothing. They were just things you wore to stop you from getting cold or arrested for indecency. We mustn't forget that.

The image of my mother's naked bottom being shoved into a police van was not something I'd ever be able to forget. Marcus's mother, whom I'd met ever so briefly at the fashion show, didn't look like the type to get herself arrested.

Chewing on my lower lip, I rang the doorbell. What would she think of my mother? They'll never meet, so what did it matter? I didn't argue with the logic.

The door opened, and a look of confusion ran over Charlie's face. "Oh, hey Fin, I wasn't expecting to see you."

"That's because he's not here to see you," Nanna shouted from down the hallway behind Charlie.

He swung to face her and shook his head. "You know you're shouting, and I'm not deaf. I also suspect Fin isn't either."

She tsked. "I wasn't shouting."

She had been. Would it be rude to point it out?

With no chance to think on the subject, I was pulled through the door. "Come, I've made some treats." Her gaze went to the bag. "Did you bring all your outfits?"

I held up the bag. "What there is of them, yes."

A furrow appeared between Charlie's brows. "Outfits?"

"We're going to help Fin pick an outfit for his date with Marcus tomorrow," Nanna announced.

"Marcus Crestwell? You're going on a date with him?" called a deep, male voice.

Charlie rolled his eyes to the ceiling. "Griffin, stop shouting. You're getting as bad as Nanna."

I didn't point out that he was also shouting. Griffin appeared in the doorway of a room I'd not been in. Did he never wear anything other than a suit? Today's was a pewter grey.

"It's the only way to be heard in this house," he answered in a gruff voice.

I didn't miss the heated looks the two men were throwing at each other, and neither did Nanna. From the way she was tugging me down the hall, I felt like she knew what was coming next. A deep moan followed, and Nanna whispered in my ear, "Griff only got back a few minutes ago. It's not safe to stay in this part of the house. Well, not unless you want to get an eyeful of men's naked bits."

I scratched at my head. "I like men's naked bits."

She patted my arm but kept on pulling me with her. "That you do and such a pity I'm not a bloke."

How nice. Did she remember I was here because of a guy I was dating? "That's very flattering. You do remember I'm dating Marcus? I think we are dating. It's hard to tell because he's not like any of my other dates. There's been no sex yet, and most of the men I've gone out with wanted sex. That usually ended up with me being dumped right after. So maybe it's a good thing Marcus isn't interested enough to get me naked."

Nanna gave my hand another pat. "Those other men were fools."

Had I just been insulted?

The door opened in front of us before the conversation could continue. Rachael appeared with Cissy at her heel. "Fucking feed me," came the demonic voice.

I eyed the big tabby. "Oh dear, poor Cissy isn't happy."

I crouched down and held out my hand, which she duly sniffed before turning and sticking her bottom high in the air. "Maybe you need to feed her before we look in the bag?"

Nanna shook her head. "Oh, laddie, don't worry about her. She's being greedy."

Rachael, who I'd learnt was Nanna's companion and, as it turned out, a partner in crime, reached for the bag I held when I stood up. "Let's have a looksie. Charlie's not the only one who can sew a stitch."

"Why would you need to sew a stitch?"

She glanced down at my clothes and tutted. "I've yet to see you in a piece of clothing, besides what the boys made for you, that doesn't have a hole in it."

"They're from charity shops," I answered, shrugging. As far back as I could remember, I'd never had anything new. Even the outfit Guy had picked for the fashion show was a cast-off.

"Being frugal is good, but there has to be something in those shops that doesn't have a hole in it?"

A wave of heat rode up my neck. "I'm not keen on shopping, so I just pick up whatever I see first."

Both women tutted this time. The bag was opened, and Nanna and Rachael groaned in unison. "This won't do," Nanna exclaimed.

Rachel glanced at Nanna. "Isn't there a pile of clothes left from the fashion show upstairs?"

Her fingers snapped together. "There is. I'll go get them while you get the sewing basket." Nanna pointed at me. "You...strip."

There was no chance to argue as I was frog marched into the large room with the view over the beach that I'd come to love. The waves were high tonight as the sun set and cast a glittering glow over the sea, giving them a hypnotic, golden shimmer.

I had no idea how long I stood staring, but soon enough, Nanna was back with an armful of clothes, and Rachel was sitting on the sofa, searching through a large, weaved basket full of coloured cotton threads.

"Are you sure Charlie won't mind you using those clothes?"

"Pfft, he'll not even notice they're gone. There are hundreds of things up there. Anyone would think he's got some sort of clothes addiction."

"Like you?" Rachael said, her smile cheeky.

Nanna ran a hand down the side of the lovely lemon blouse she was wearing and sighed. "After all those years of scrimping and keeping that good for nothing husband of mine, I'm entitled to splurge occasionally."

Rachael coughed and muttered behind her hand, "Occasionally." Her brows rose. "Is that like the Pope choosing to be Catholic only on Sundays?"

I chuckled, getting the joke as Nanna carried on as if Rachael hadn't spoken.

"Look at this pair of trousers. These might work." She glanced at me and frowned. "Why aren't you naked?"

Seeing that it was futile to argue, I stripped out of what I was wearing, leaving on my underwear, also secondhand.

Nanna visibly paled as she came forward, her eyes on my crotch. "Where the heck, laddie, did you get those?"

I glanced down at the Batman underwear. Hadn't I already explained where I shop? "In a shop."

"What shop?" she questioned, in a tone that left me a little confused.

"The same shop where I buy everything."

Her squeal was loud enough to make my eardrums ring.

"Dear lordy. You buy," she shuddered, her eyes widening, "secondhand underwear?"

I nodded carefully, getting the distinct impression I'd somehow made a misstep by admitting to where I'd bought my underwear.

"No. That is wrong on so many levels. Put your clothes back on. We're going shopping."

A flare of panic followed as Rachael stood and nodded. "I think that lovely lady that owns the little underwear boutique opens late on a Friday."

"I don't have money for new clothes." I pointed to the pants that seemed to have caused offence, not that I could see anything wrong with them. Maybe they didn't like Batman? "These are perfectly suitable. There aren't any holes in them. Besides the ones you need. You know, to go to the toilet and for your legs." I was rambling, and I couldn't seem to make myself stop as Nanna approached me with a determined expression.

"There'll be no arguments. Are you my friend?"

Again, was this a trick question? "Yes, I'd like to think so."

She took hold of my hand and squeezed. "Friend to friend, no one should ever have to wear secondhand underwear." I opened my mouth then shut it when she rose just one brow, a move my mother often pulled on me to shut me up. "I understand money is tight for you. I've been in that situation, so I know how hard it is. Griff changed many things for me, and I like to share that generosity around."

This time I couldn't stop myself from saying something. "Nanna…" One hard stare, and I caved, clamping my lips closed.

"You'll learn there is no point arguing with her," Rachael stated, with more glee than the situation warranted. At least, it did, in my opinion.

I found myself inside a fancy boutique no more than an hour later, with a pile of underwear in a shiny carrier bag and no clue how I'd pay for it. The number of zeros on the receipt made me sweat.

As we left the shop, I tried once more to argue that one pair for a date—that might or might not end in sex—was all I'd really needed if my others weren't suitable. "Nanna, I don't need all these." Why did that sound more like a question?

"You do because you're going to go home and throw all the old ones away." She glanced at the car at the curb that Rachael had driven.

Her hand went to her chin, her eyes narrowing. "In fact, I think we'll go back to your home and help you get rid of them."

Was she a mind reader? Did she know I'd no intention of throwing perfectly good clothes out?

I got in the car and sighed, resigned to the fact I wasn't going to get a say. "You should meet my mother. You're very alike."

Nanna settled in the front seat, then looked back at me. "What a lovely compliment. I'd love to meet her. You'll need to arrange it."

"Are you sure?" No one ever wanted to purposefully meet my mother. "She lives in a tepee in the woods."

"How adventurous of her, and of course I want to meet her. In fact, after we've got rid of all your underwear, we'll figure out a good time to visit your Ma. I've never been in a tepee before."

I only felt it fair to warn them about the bathroom facilities. "You have to go to the bathroom in a hole in the ground."

Rachael made a choking noise, and Nanna chuckled. "As long as nothing tries to bite my arse, I'll be fine." She gave a girlish giggle. "That is unless it's some hunky silver fox, then he can bite away."

"There aren't any silver foxes in the UK. You'll only find those in North America," I pointed out helpfully.

Nanna and Rachael laughed loudly. I grinned and sat back in my seat. It was nice to see that I'd put their minds at ease.

CHAPTER ELEVEN

Marcus

The drive to Brighton was uneventful, and traffic had been kind, so I made it in good time. I followed the sat nav's directions, which led me down a street full of terraced houses. Seeing no place to park, I drove around for several minutes, starting to sweat as the time ticked away.

"Shit! Why is there never a place to park when you need one?" Giving up on the hope of finding a spot close to Fin's home, I parked several streets away.

Out of the car, I pulled out my phone and dialled Fin. I started talking the second the phone connected. "Hey, sorry, I couldn't find a place to park."

"Oh. Is that why you're late?"

"Yeah, I should be with you in about five minutes."

"Why are you walking to me?"

"Why wouldn't I walk to you? I couldn't park outside your house," I explained, thinking he might have misunderstood me.

"Wouldn't it have made more sense to just get me to walk to your car?" I could hear movement and a shutting door through the phone. "I'll walk to you. Where exactly are you?"

I grinned and looked about. "No clue. Wait for me where you are because I know how to get there."

"Can't you read road signs?" he asked, sounding worried.

"I can, but I can't see any near where I am right now." We carried on the conversation right up until I turned the corner at the end of his road and waved at him.

As I got a load of what he was wearing, my step faltered. His concern about the dress code for tonight popped into my head, right along with the worry he'd gone out and spent money on what looked like designer clothes.

The charcoal grey trousers were cut to suggest they were expensive, but they clung to all the right parts of him, enhancing the length of his leg without making them look too thin. He'd paired them with a mint green shirt, which fitted in a way that made me want to run my hands over him. The whole ensemble was completed with the same Doc Martins he'd had on the last time I'd seen him and a jacket the same colour as the trousers hung from the fingers of one hand. He'd even managed to style his hair, sort of. It wasn't pointing in several different directions, which is about as close to style as he could probably manage. Fuck he looked...hot.

To distract me, I glanced down, seeing no overnight bag. I chuckled, recalling what he'd deemed appropriate for a night away from home that very first day I'd met him. "You scrub up well. I hope you didn't blow your budget on new clothes for today?" I aimed for humour, despite wishing he'd not blown whatever cash he had. How did one go about asking about other people's money situation?

An adorable wrinkle appeared between his brows as he glanced down, then back at me. "I'm not sure scrubbing these clothes is a good thing. They might not survive. They're so flimsy. And that would be a shame as Nanna and Rachael went to so much effort to make sure they fit properly."

Okay, he'd lost me. "You look gorgeous. It was meant as a compliment. But what do Nanna and Racheal have to do with your clothes?"

"It was?" His cheeks grew pink while he shuffled on the spot.

God, I wanted to kiss him. I shoved my hands into my trouser pockets to stop myself from reaching for him, not sure he'd like to be kissed on the street in daylight. I glanced at the house he was standing in front of. "Do you need to grab anything else?"

He shook his head. "I'm ready."

Curious, I had to ask, "You don't need an overnight bag?"

A grin spread over his face, and my stomach flipped. He held up his jacket and waved it. "I've everything I need here. The new underwear is pretty small, so it fits in a pocket, which leaves the other one for my toiletries." He sounded so pleased with himself, but I got stuck on the underwear comment.

Intrigued, I took hold of his free hand and clasped it loosely in mine. His gaze moved to our hands. "Is this all right?" I lifted our joined hands.

"Yeah. I'm just not used to it. No one's ever wanted to hold my hand before you. Except for my mum, that would have been weird if she'd not wanted to do that. I was a child at the time." He shrugged. "Although, she might not have wanted to hold my hand. I'd never thought about that. She probably did it to keep me from running off. I did that a lot."

The rambling was starting to make sense to me, and I wasn't sure what that said about what was happening between us. I left it alone for now and went back to the subject of his underwear. "New underwear? Did you treat yourself?"

We started walking back in the direction of my car.

"No."

The grin spread wider over my face. "Did someone else treat you?"

The wrinkle was back. "Is it a treat if you don't have any say when someone insists that your underwear needs to go in the bin and wants to replace what you have with new stuff?"

The genuine seriousness left me thinking about my answer. "Was it a gift?" He nodded. "Then I'd say that could be classed as a treat. But I'm gonna have to ask, why would someone want to throw out all your underwear and replace it?"

He stopped and stared at me. "I knew you'd understand."

I chuckled. "Understand what, Fin?"

"That secondhand underwear is perfectly okay. Nanna was insistent it wasn't. That's why I've new underwear. She took me shopping last night." He shook his head. "She's very bossy, did you know that?"

My eyes widened. "Nanna bought you underwear because all yours was secondhand?"

"Isn't that what I just said." His brows rose.

I kept hold of my laughter because of the gravity of his expression. "You did. I'm sorry."

I started walking again, trying to remember a time before Fin when I'd had this much fun on a date. "So does Nanna have good taste in underwear?"

"She likes skimpy things," he said, a strangled noise escaping from him as his face flushed with bright colour. "And things that are...sexy. I'm not so sure I can make anything look sexy, but she was insistent."

It was a struggle not to get him to explain exactly what he meant by sexy. "Women tend to have a strong opinion on what they like to see on a man when it comes to underwear."

"You got that right," he sighed. "I've tried to tell her I only like boys. I think sometimes she can be a little forgetful."

That woman was no more forgetful than my mother, but I didn't point that out. Turning up the next street, I pointed to the car. "Here we are."

His lips twitched into a smile. "You drive a hybrid?"

"Yep, I did a little research when I decided to convert over. The Audi e-Tron GT can go two-hundred-ninety-six miles between charges, so it's a good car to have when I need to travel to different parts of the country. Everyone should do their bit for the environment." There were other measures I'd taken to conserve energy in my home. I'd also have had a wind turbine on the land at the back of my house if I'd been able to get planning permission for it. I cared about the planet, and I hoped that some of the things I did to damage it were counterbalanced by the other ways I tried to help. As humans, we all produce carbon, so it was a hard thing to get right.

"This is true. Nanna wouldn't let me recycle my old underwear."

The laughter was out before I could stop it at the 'woe is me' expression on his face. I hugged him. "Nanna can be a force of nature...but maybe this time she was..." He peered up at me through his dark eyelashes, and I lost my train of thought. The need won over my good intentions, and I lowered my mouth to his. I paused to give him a chance to move away. When he blinked slowly but remained where he was, I removed the couple of inches separating us.

The memory and worry about that first chaste kiss were removed as his soft, and plump lips pressed firmly against mine. There was the taste of mint as his lips parted, and he moaned as my tongue touched his. My arms tightened around him, and his heady scent enveloped me. His body melted against mine, and I groaned when a hand caressed my back. I was vaguely aware of the warmth of the sun on my head and the sounds of traffic, but it was Fin that held my attention.

He fitted against me like a missing part I'd not been aware had been absent. The tightening arousal at my groin left me breathless and struggling to ignore the temptation to strip off Fin's clothing and...

Nope, you're in the street. What happened to your polished moves?

I gently untangled myself from him after one last kiss. Stepping back, Fin stared at me with heavy-lidded eyes that didn't help my trouser situation at all. Searching for my key fob, I opened the car and kept my distance from the silent, tempting man.

He followed suit and got in the car. He cast me several glances as he buckled up, and I started the engine.

"You okay?" I asked, not looking at him as I concentrated on the road and pulled out of the parking space. My hands gripped the steering wheel until my knuckles were white as the seconds ticked by with no reply.

"I've never been kissed like that."

With a wildly beating heart, I gave him a quick glance. "Like what?"

He rubbed at his lips. "With care."

The ball forming in my throat made it difficult to swallow. "How have you been kissed before?" Was that too personal?

"It tended to be rough. Not sexy rough, but like they were in a rush and couldn't really be bothered. It was all a bit wet and sloppy, not that I ever told them. Is it bad that I'm saying that to you? I've always wondered if I picked men that had some sort of saliva production problem."

Evidently not too personal. I bit my lower lip hard to stop from laughing at his description and did my best to pretend my ego hadn't grown several sizes bigger. "Maybe we should practice some more, just to make sure it wasn't a fluke?"

He shifted in his seat and looked at me fully. "Practice? What would that entail? Is this like a science project?"

I glanced at him, noting that the furrow was back. Fuck I wanted to kiss him again. "If you like. Though I'll warn you, I'm a perfectionist and like to practice *a lot*."

The smile that appeared lit up his face and smoothed his brow. "I think the kiss was flawless... but if you feel the need to practice, I'll be willing to help out."

There was a lot about him that attracted me, but flirty Fin was irresistible. "You want to be my science partner?" I joked.

"No one's ever wanted to partner with me before. I'd like that."

The simple honesty brought back the lump in my throat, only this time there was also anger at all those who hadn't seen what a wonderful person he was. I worked to keep the tone light. "Then you're stuck with me."

"I'm sure that won't last very long," he mumbled and went back to looking out the window.

There was something in the way he said it that made me want to show him just how wrong he was. Letting the topic drop, my mind already in turmoil, I started to chat about Steve.

CHAPTER TWELVE

Fin

We'd been at the party two hours, and at some point, Marcus had got separated from me when Steve had wanted to introduce him to someone. That had left me with the man in front of me who talked *non-stop*. I wasn't even sure he'd drawn breath since he'd started. Did he like the sound of his own voice? None of what he was talking about was in the least bit interesting. Politeness had kept me there, even though my attention had wandered over to Marcus on the other side of the room.

Dressed much the same as he'd been every other time I'd seen him, he wore black jeans, though these were a little more distressed looking. The shirt was charcoal grey, and he'd rolled up the sleeves to reveal tanned forearms. One wrist held a watch, but the other had several leather bands that were…sexy.

I licked at my lips. The tingling from our kiss had long since passed, but the odd sensation in the pit of my stomach lingered. I'd been attracted to men before, but Marcus's kiss had revealed something to me. Desire, it came, it would seem, in many different levels of intensity. What I'd felt with the other men would have maybe been a two, possibly a three. Marcus didn't have a level I could put into words. All I knew was the desire that had pulsed through me earlier was a new experience. One I wanted to repeat.

On the other side of the room, Marcus moved away from a striking blond guy who kept putting his hand on Marcus's forearm. The hand dropped away, the smile on Marcus's face remained. Was it the same one he gave me? No, I didn't think so. Those smiles reached his eyes. The one aimed at the blond did not.

Why wasn't the blond noticing?

The hand came back up and stroked at Marcus's forearm once more. "If you'll excuse me," I muttered, not giving the man, whose name I couldn't remember, a chance to start on again about…whatever he was talking about. I was doing the guy a favour really, at least he'd have a chance to take a decent breath.

Marcus's smile deepened when I stopped in front of him and the blond. "Why do you keep touching Marcus?"

The silence that followed was...I wasn't sure, maybe a little tense where the blond was concerned. Marcus continued to give me a smile that reached his eyes.

"*Excuse me?* Do you know how rude you're being right now?" The blond's gaze narrowed on me.

Crap. I scratched at my head. Had I been rude? Possibly. But he'd been touching Marcus continually for the last ten minutes. "Is it any ruder than you constantly touching my date?"

Marcus made a sort of choking noise before he coughed into his hand.

The blond glared at me, his gaze moving over me before rejecting whatever he saw. He moved his body as if to block me from the conversation and his brows, which had been plucked to death, rose at Marcus. "The guy has to be delusional. You can't possibly be dating...*him*."

Relaxed, Marcus disappeared so fast it could have given me whiplash as he repositioned himself so his arm could drape around my waist. I was gently tugged into the side of his body as he unceremoniously pushed the blond away from us. "Delusional?

How so, Jimmy?" he asked in a tone that would have frozen hell. Jimmy's face flushed an ugly red, seemingly unable to answer Marcus. "Fin *is* my date. And there is nothing delusional about how I feel around him." As if to make his point, he kissed me.

His lips brushed over mine, and I lost my ability to think about the blond or anything else for that matter. Sweetness and masculinity were all I could taste as Marcus encouraged me to part my lips. His tongue delved into my mouth, and I moaned when it stroked over mine as it had done earlier. My toes curled in my boots.

When he finally lifted his head, the blond had disappeared, and I was breathless. "You ready to leave?"

At the arousal pressed against my side, any idea about being sensible disappeared. "Leave, yeah." It was the best I could manage when my body and brain weren't cooperating. Was I acting like a dork? Steve and his boyfriend gave me several odd looks while I stood mute and Marcus made our excuses. Minutes later, we were back in his car and on the way home.

Marcus's hand rested on my thigh, his face shadowed by the darkness of the night. "I've a spare room."

"What?" I blinked, turning to look sideways. Didn't he want sex? Had I misunderstood?

"I'm saying that sex is not expected. That the choice is yours, and I've a spare room if you want to stay in there tonight." His tone was utterly serious.

"Do you want sex?"

He groaned. "Fuck yeah. But I also want you to understand that it's not expected. That I'll go at your pace, whatever that might be."

The hand on my thigh pressed a little firmer, and he glanced at me briefly. "I like you. I want to see where we are going."

"Then you'd best look at the road."

"God, I wish I could kiss you right now," he said through his laughter.

"I wouldn't recommend that. You would crash, and how would you explain that to the police?" I asked in all seriousness. Was he prone to taking risks like that?

"Fin…" His laughter seemed to stop him from being able to say more.

Maybe it was safer to keep quiet?

Concentrating on keeping silent, I stared out the car window, watching to see where we were headed. Canary wharf came into view, and I tried to memorise which way we were headed. The house we eventually stopped outside of was…huge. "Aren't we going back to yours?"

"This is my house and technically my place of work."

"You own this?" I said, staring up at what appeared to be a vast, four-storey property. There was no way he couldn't have heard the incredulity in my voice.

"Yes, own it." He twisted to face me, his hand moving to take hold of the one closest to him. "Let's just get this out of the way. I'm rich, I said this before, but I may have missed off the crazy part. I don't want to be crass, but there are a lot of zeros in my bank balance."

Money had never been something that really bothered me or been something I gave a lot of thought to. It only really came up when it came to paying for things, and then I thought about it a lot. Usually while I weighed up the decision to spend what I had.

"That's nice." I wasn't really sure what to say to Marcus, so I opted for that, hoping it would put an end to the conversation.

He chuckled. "It is. Shall we go in?"

I nodded and unclipped my seatbelt. Once more, he took my hand as we walked up to the front of the house. He did something with his thumb and pressed several buttons before he put his key into the lock. Inside, the air was filled with the fresh scent that I associated with clean bed linen. As far as I could see, the floors were all wooden and appeared to be the original floorboards. It was the walls that held my attention, though, covered in framed photos. Some I recognised from the book I'd borrowed, others I'd seen on the internet. What drew my gaze were the black-and-white images. They were stark, and some were brutal, but they were powerful and full of emotion.

"Where were these taken?" It was only when I glanced at Marcus that I noticed how far I walked down the hall to get a closer look.

"Sarajevo." His face revealed none of his thoughts, but there was a wealth of pain in that one word.

"Were you there during the fighting?" I slapped my forehead. "Don't answer that. It was a stupid question. The picture speaks for itself."

He came closer, his fingers brushing over where I'd slapped myself, his gaze holding mine. "I'd prefer it if you didn't hit yourself." His lips took the same path as his fingertips.

"The only way I want to see your skin pink is from something a little more pleasurable," he murmured against my warming skin.

"There is lots of research to suggest spanking can be very pleasurable," I responded.

One brow quirked up at me as he gave me a little breathing room. "Is that so?" His lips hovered over mine.

Flustered by the desire he revealed, I nodded, thinking that was best as all moisture suddenly left my mouth.

His voice deepened to a husky rasp. "We'll maybe revisit that, but right now," he lips brushed mine, once, twice, "do you think you'd be interested in me stripping off your clothes and seeing if I can make your skin flush from something else?"

I nodded once more. The last thing I wanted to try was talking, when my mind was running way ahead, and I wasn't sure whatever came out of my mouth would make any sense. The desire from the second kiss returned at Marcus's gentle touches. He guided me up two flights of stairs, past yet more photos that I hoped to get the chance to look at later.

The light he turned on when we stopped at the side of a huge bed that could easily fit a family of five glowed over the rich colours in the room. In the main, everything was navy, burgundy and cream. The place was neat and tidy.

Warmth pressed to my back, and the scent of Marcus's aftershave was all I could smell. The woody fragrance suited him. "Will you let me strip off your clothes."

His mouth trailed down the side of my neck, hot breath heating the skin, while his stubble tickled me and sent shivers of pleasure to run through me. Large hands sat low on my hips. "Can I?"

"Can you what?"

His chuckle blew over my neck. "Strip you out of those clothes?"

Oh yeah, he'd asked me a question. How was I supposed to remember my own name when he was touching me like this? "Yes," I gasped as he nibbled on my jaw.

My eyes drifted closed while his hands moved up the front of my shirt. One after another, the buttons were opened. Fingertips stroked over the skin, he revealed.

"Your skin is so smooth, do you wax?"

I shuddered with the feel of fingertips squeezing my nipples, and my head lolled on Marcus's shoulder. Question, he asked a question. Why did he keep doing that?

"No waxing." It was the best I could manage with his hands and mouth doing delicious things to me.

"God, you're so responsive," he murmured as I gave another full-body shudder.

"It's you," I panted, groaning at the erection pushing into the crease of my backside.

"How so?"

"No one...oh shit...that." It didn't make much sense, but it was my best answer when one hand dropped to the front of my trousers and squeezed my cock gently.

There was more laughter, but he wasn't laughing at me, more with me, I think. It was hard to tell when his hands were teasing and touching me.

His mouth was next to my ear, his tongue tracing the lobe, which he bit gently. "What do you like?"

The way my cock was reacting, couldn't he tell? No one had ever asked me before, so how was I supposed to answer? The hand that had started to stroke over my cock stopped, and I groaned in distress. "Why are you stopping?"

Who was the whiny person?

You!

He stepped in front of me, and I looked up to meet his gaze. His face was as flushed as I felt. The light dancing in his eyes was dark and just a little dangerous. "I want to make this good for you."

As if to prove his point, he took off my shirt and went back to stroking over my skinny chest. "Your body is all angles. It's beautiful." The way he spoke, with reverence, his eyes alight with desire, left me unable to argue. "I want you to feel special."

Exhaling a shuddery breath, I stepped back. His hands dropped to his sides, his brow pinched. "I can't think when you touch me," I explained. "You keep asking me things and expect me to answer. It's maybe best if you get all the questions out now, and then I won't have to try and think."

His lower lip quivered before he bit it, but his eyes danced with humour. Again, not the kind that was cruel or demeaning. I grinned at him. "You think I'm funny. It's okay, I can be."

"Fin...you are such a breath of fresh air."

"There really is no such thing as fresh air, not with the amount of pollution around..."

His hands cupped my face, and a second later, he was kissing me. Firm lips pressed to mine as potent as they'd been every other time he'd kissed me. With his hands holding me, all I could do was follow his lead. His tongue touched the seam of my lips, and I opened. His taste flooded my mouth as he deepened the kiss, his moan low and needy as he angled my head. Hands moved from my cheeks to slide into my hair. I shifted forward as much as his hold would allow, and my hands slid up the front of his shirt. All instinct, the desire so strong it was easy to lose myself to it. Unbuttoning his shirt, the soft, springy hair beneath was a delight. I whimpered as I ran my hands over the naked muscles. Fuck, he was all solid muscle and hair.

I wasn't sure how it happened, but the next thing I was on the bed, minus my clothes, and Marcus was pressing me into the soft mattress, his naked chest rubbing against mine. Flares of lust spread through my body, and I thrust up, disappointed to find Marcus's trousers still in place. "Naked," I gasped against his mouth.

"You're naked." As if to prove his point, his hand slipped down the side of my body until it got to my hip, and he lifted away from me to take hold of my cock. A firm squeeze was followed by a caress from base to tip. The precum he found was used to tease the head of my cock. His fingertips slicked over the sensitive flesh in swirling motions, tormenting me while his mouth teased mine with drugging kisses. My hips thrust up in search of more. Were those noises coming from me?

The level of my desperation was not something I was used to, and I couldn't figure out how to tell him to get naked and stop teasing me. Not that I wanted him to stop teasing, it really was amazing and something I hoped he'd continue.

The hand working my cock increased the speed of its strokes as Marcus released my lips to kiss his way over my collarbone and down to my left nipple.

"Gorgeous." Moaning, he bit my nipple just as he stroked up my cock and his hand did this twisty thing. Bright and bold sensations flooded through me, quickly followed by a tingling that travelled through my cock and connected to my nipple.

One more sharp pinch with his teeth, and I cried out. "Bollocks…"

The rest got stuck in my throat as it closed under the grip of the most stunning orgasm. Shudder after shudder rippled through me, leaving me panting and sweaty by the time I collapsed bonelessly on the bed.

"I wish I had my camera to capture how you look right now."

Only as Marcus spoke did I realise I'd shut my eyes. They fired open, leaving the room fuzzy for a moment. "You can't be serious."

Marcus was so close I could see his expression clearly.

"Deadly. You're beautiful." His fingers stroked down the side of my sweaty face. "The lines and angles of your body are stunningly beautiful. It makes it almost impossible for me to not go and grab my camera." His lips followed the path of his fingers. The erection pressed against my thigh became my focus as he moved.

"Do you want me—"

"What I want right now is to just lie here and cuddle with you. Is that all right?" he asked.

There was a hint of uncertainty I'd never heard in his voice before. I searched his face, but it revealed nothing. Did he think I wanted to cuddle? No one, not even my mum, had cuddled me before. Would I like it?

"If you want." It was the best I could come up with.

He shifted, looking at his sticky hand before rubbing it on his trouser leg. Then he reached over me to tug the duvet from under us. Once he'd settled the cover over us, he slipped an arm under my body to position me against his side, my head on his shoulder. Assessing the position, I grinned at how comfy it was. "I like this."

He kissed the top of my head. "Me too."

CHAPTER THIRTEEN

Marcus

An unfamiliar sound and a hiss alerted me to the fact that I wasn't alone. As my brain attempted to wake up, I shifted and groaned. Why did I still have my trousers on?

Fin.

I blinked sleepily and reached out to find the bed empty. The sheets were warm, but as my gaze swept the room, I found it empty as well. My heart thudded against my ribs as I sat up and pushed off the cover to swing my legs to the floor. The curtains were shut, but the lamp I'd switched on last night was still on.

Last night came flooding back and reminded me why I had a patch of cum flaking kept on to make sure that what happened between us had been all about the man who'd come apart from the attention I'd given him. The wonderment on Fin's face had been worth holding back my own needs. He was special in so many ways, and I'd wanted to show him that what was happening between us wasn't just a quick fuck. Half expecting a flare of panic, I wasn't overly surprised when the overall feeling I had was anticipation. Fin had a way about him that reminded me what was important in life.

There was a loud snuffling sound coming from the open door. What was he doing?

I got up to investigate. Fin was stood in just his trousers about six feet from the door, staring at a photo hanging on the wall. Tears were tracking down his face and dripping down onto the wooden floor. He didn't appear to notice as he sniffed, then used the back of a hand to wipe over the end of his nose.

He took a sidestep to look at the next picture. The three pictures I'd had framed were of a family I'd met while they'd been alive. The first photo showed the mother, father, and two daughters laughing. The room wasn't anything special, but the picture was all about the love between them. They were one of the many families my foundation helped to rebuild their lives after their homes had been bombed in a senseless war they didn't choose to be a part of. After taking that picture, I'd left them with a plan to visit again before I travelled home.

Pain sliced at me as I took in the images that followed. I sucked in a deep, shaky breath. It was the same every time I looked at them. Steve had asked why I'd framed and hung these pictures when they caused me pain. That was easy. It was to remind me of how precious life was. On my return visit, I'd found the family dead. Militants had come in the night and killed many men, women, and children.

Fin reached up and traced a finger over the child that lay in her bed, covered in her own blood and that of her mother, who lay half over her. It looked as if she'd tried to protect the child. It was a powerful image of a mothers love.

"It hurts," he whispered.

I wasn't sure if he was talking to me or just talking aloud. "It does," I answered anyway.

Tear drenched eyes stared at me. "Do you carry them with you?"

That he'd ask that, when no one else ever had, showed the kind of person he was. "Yes, every one of them." I touched my bare chest and rubbed over my thudding heart. "How could I not?"

He glanced back at the picture. "These images are the history we will leave behind for those who come after us. They're important." He looked back at me. "They matter."

The ache at the back of my eyes and thickness developing in my throat left me nodding, unsure I'd be able to talk without breaking.

Fin walked to me and laid his head on my chest, his arms going around my waist. "You can hold on to me if it helps."

A tear slid down my cheek, then another. Before I realised it, I was crying. I buried my face in his sweet, scented hair and breathed him in. He remained silent, holding me as the years of holding in the horrors I'd encountered poured out of me. The dam that broke ensured his hair was more than a little damp by the time I lifted my head.

His smile was sweet, and any thoughts of being embarrassed by the show of emotion disappeared. "Is there anything I can do?"

I stroked a finger down the side of his face. "No..." I hesitated to figure out how I was feeling. "This was actually just what I needed." And it was. The bogged down feeling when it came to my work that I'd had since my last trip had lifted. "Do you have any plans for today?"

He nodded. "I wasn't sure if you'd kick me out this morning, so I agreed to have lunch with Nanna and Rachael. I think they just want to know how the date went. They seem awfully keen on knowing all the details about everything."

"They're a pair, that's for sure. You up for me gate crashing your lunch date?" I ask, grinning.

A pink flush covered his cheeks. "You aren't kicking me out?"

I kissed him because, why not?

His lips responded and pressed firmly against mine for a second, then he pulled back so fast he nearly lost his balance. I reached out to steady him. "What's wrong?"

"Morning breath, I haven't brushed my teeth," He said, by way of explanation as he backed further away from me.

I followed, a grin reappearing on my face. "I've morning breath too." His back hit the wall behind him, leaving him nowhere to go. I placed my hands on either side of his head and leant in to brush my lips over his. "Would you deny me a kiss?"

He shivered, his lower lip quivering as I nipped at it. Eyes wide, his pupils grew so big the colour of his eyes vanished. He slowly shook his head. Not needing a second invite, I dipped in and kissed him deep and hard. The only part of our bodies touching was our lips. The power of that simple touch left me aching for more. "What time do we need to be in Brighton for?"

"Twelve," he murmured against my mouth, his lips chasing mine.

I glanced sideways and twisted my wrist to check the time. Groaning in disappointment, I looked back at the sexy man chewing on his lower lip. "I want so badly to explore your body...but for that, I need more than fifteen minutes."

The eyes were back to wide. "Really? The other guys were done with me..." he scratched at his cheek. "I can't recall accurately, but it was less than fifteen minutes." He looked so damn serious.

"Fucking fools." I pressed a quick kiss to his far too tempting mouth. "Rest assured I'm not foolish, and I will need hours to find out all the secrets of your body."

His breath rushed out over my face. "Oh."

Stepping back was far harder than it had ever been with any other man I'd been with. I pointed back to my bedroom door. "Go use my bathroom. I'll use the main one. You should find everything you need in there." I grinned at him, recalling where we'd left his jacket. "You left your overnight bag in the car."

Frown lines appeared between his brows. "I didn't bring an overnight bag, so how did I leave it in the car?" I waited a few more seconds, and a slow smile spread over his face. "You mean my jacket."

My grin matched his. "That I do."

"It's got my underwear in it."

"You could go commando?"

The horrified look that flew across his face was priceless, and I was laughing before he started to babble. "Nanna, Racheal, oh no, that would be...I'm not sure what it would be, but Nanna is like a hunting dog. She'll sniff out the fact I'm wearing any pants. Not that I'm smelly or anything. I've never had that problem, although there was this one incident with a skunk when my mum took me to a commune. But I prefer not to talk about that."

"A skunk?"

He buried his head in his hands, then peeked out between his fingers. "You really don't want to know."

"I want to know everything about you." The hands fell away from his face, his lips parted, but he made no sound. I swooped in for another kiss, then stepped back from temptation. "If you continue to stand there all tempting, I'm going to forget the lunch plans."

As if in a stupor, he shook his head twice before he walked back in the direction of my bedroom, his arse holding my attention before he disappeared. I adjusted my cock and cursed as I walked off to the other bathroom.

Within the hour, we were in the car, Fin in his underwear that I'd had to retrieve from the car for him. Had I peeked in the pocket, maybe? The guy was far too tempting, and I could see the distance between London and Brighton might become a little bit of a pain with how much I wanted to be with him.

"Why did you choose photography?"

I glanced sideways, then back to the busy motorway. "It wasn't a case of me choosing it, more the other way around. The second I picked up my grandfather's Canon that he'd brought to my seventh birthday, when I looked through the lens, it changed the perspective of my world."

Fin shifted in his seat, twisting more so he was facing me rather than the windscreen. "Do you still have the first picture you took?"

I laughed. "I do. It's in my studio."

"I think you mentioned that your studio is in your home?"

"It is. Next time you come over, I'll take you down there. I really want to do a photoshoot with you on your own." There was a choked noise coming from the seat next to me, and I shifted my attention to Fin for a second. His face revealed his scepticism. "Why do you doubt how attractive you are?"

"Because I have a mirror and it isn't like the mirror in *Snow White and the Huntsman*. Not that I'm comparing myself to Charlize Theron, she was nasty in that film, and no one wants to be a murderer sucking the life out of others to keep your beauty. Okay, maybe some would. Otherwise, why would there be so many people having plastic surgery to make themselves look younger? Only they don't always look younger...just pinched and tight. How are you supposed to read someone when their face doesn't move?" He shifted in his seat, looking back out the front window.

When I caught his expression, it was one I was starting to recognise. It was one that said he thought he'd gone on a ramble for too long, so I reached out to reassure him. "That makes sense. Only seven percent of communication is verbal. If you take away facial expressions, we're doomed to misinterpretation."

I was rewarded with a shy smile that left a fuzzy feeling in the centre of my chest. One I wasn't stupid enough to want to think about right now while I was driving. No, I'd need to think about that...alone and without the tempting man sat next to me.

CHAPTER FOURTEEN

Fin

The last thing I'd expected was for Marcus to want to come to lunch. However, I was coming to realise nothing of what Marcus did followed any kind of pattern, which for some reason suited me just fine. He had a way about him that didn't make me feel small or stupid when I started to ramble. This was a new concept and one I was fast growing to…

What was this I was feeling? Love? Or was it just lust? My mother had often said there was no such thing as love. It was only lust, then the shine wore off. I'd really hoped she was wrong, but up to now, I'd never experienced anything that I'd give a name to.

To distract me as we reached the outskirts of Brighton, I gave Marcus the pub's address that we were going to meet Nanna and Rachael in. I listened as the sat nav told us to take the next turning on the right. "How do you think that box can process information and know exactly where to take you when my head struggles to recall how to get from the bed to the bathroom some days."

The rich sound of Marcus's laugher, something he did a lot, filled the car as he followed the instructions. "I try hard not to think about big brother."

My nose wrinkled. "*Big Brother*? I haven't watched that series on channel four. I think it was a little before my time? How old are you?"

His laughter turned to choking as he indicated to pull into the car park next to the pub. The second he turned off the engine and twisted to look at me, I lost whatever thoughts were in my head. His laughter lines only enhanced his features, and he had these shards of light in his eyes that made them look otherworldly. "What are you doing with me?"

His hand came up to cup my cheek. "What do you think I'm doing with you?"

"I don't know. You are...you're lucky I've lost my words. You do that to me."

His thumb traced over my cheekbone. "I'm attracted to you. There is something special about you. What you see in the mirror isn't a reflection of who you are, Fin. It's what's inside a person that counts, but beauty is truly in the eye of the beholder, and you are beautiful to me." Colour flooded his face, and there was an intensity to his gaze that held all my attention.

"I'm not sure what I'm supposed to say," I answered honestly because how was a person supposed to respond to being told they were special?

"You don't have to say anything. All you need to know is I never say anything I don't mean." He leant in and kissed me gently. It was becoming one of my most favourite things. The soft brush of his warm lips left me tingling and feeling more alive than a trip on a roller coaster at Alton Towers.

The loud tapping to the glass window next to me broke the spell. "Cooeee. You boys planning on getting out of the car? Or are you going to be introducing us to dogging? I've heard it can be quite entertaining," Nanna shouted through the closed window.

Heat seared my skin, and Marcus didn't look any better as we both looked out of the window at the street full of people now paying the car way more attention than was normal. Nanna offered an unrepentant grin while Rachael simply smiled, seeming unfazed by the fact Nanna had just been shouting about...

There was a pregnant pause then Marcus roared with laughter. "She's killer."

"She's something," I mumbled, starting to see that maybe Charlie had a point about how Nanna never thought about what she said. Wasn't I the same? "Dogging...did she mean—"

"The non-walking kind of dog activity, yep, that's exactly what Agnes meant." Marcus released my seatbelt before his own and got out of the car.

I looked at the seatbelt, then to the man now walking to the curb. An emotion that I was starting to get used to, but remained nameless, clutched at my heart.

The door next to me was opened, and Nanna's head appeared. "Come on, laddie, I'm starved, and this place does a great Sunday roast." With that, she tugged me out of the car before I could do more than nod. I'd rung earlier to warn her that Marcus was coming too, not that she'd seemed in the least bit surprised.

We were sat at a table minutes later when Nanna looked at me, a gleam in her eyes that left me shifting in my seat. "Didn't you have time to go and get changed?"

"Agnes, leave the poor boy alone. Clearly, he stayed over at Marcus's last night. Isn't that right, dearie?"

Simply for something to do, I picked up the menu as I nodded. Did Marcus want people to know I'd spent the night with him? My other dates, they'd been picky about people knowing. I glanced sideways at the man who was looking at his own menu before I returned my attention to the two women sat opposite us. "I've got clean underwear on."

Marcus choked, whereas Nanna beamed. "Was it the cute little pink jockstrap with the navy band? That one looked so good on you."

There were more choking sounds, and Marcus's shoulder moved against mine repeatedly. I chanced a glance in his direction. The mirth was there to see as he struggled to contain his laughter.

"Did you do a parade in your underwear for Agnes?" Marcus said, around his choked laughter.

"He did. He was such a good sport. The secondhand underwear had to go." Nanna gave me a stern look. "And you won't be going back to that old habit, will you?"

I tried not to shrink under her stare. "Secondhand clothes help the environment. Upcycling is a good thing, Nanna."

"Not when it comes to things that have been rubbing against your sexy parts."

The waitress, who thought it was a good time to take our order, wore a comical expression as she looked between Nanna and me. "What do you think lassie, would you want to put on someone else's underwear?"

The girl didn't seem phased. An impish smile appeared, and she tapped her pen on her lower lip. "Now, that would depend."

Marcus placed his menu down, giving the girl his full attention. "On what?"

"If it was my girlfriend's or not. I wear hers. Though I suppose size matters." Her gaze appraised the two of us. "It's not like you two could share underwear, is it?"

"I'd like to see them try," Nanna interjected, making the waitress laugh.

"I'm sure that would be fun if that was my bag."

Wrinkles deepened on Nanna's brow. "Two men swapping underwear, that's everyone's bag, surely? What do you think, Marcus, you're the photographer?"

The loud squeal was almost deafening, and several people turned to see what the commotion was. The waitress bounced on the spot. "You aren't Marcus Crestwell, are you?"

"Guilty."

"Holy cow. I can't believe this. I'm a huge fan."

It took twenty minutes, and the waitress's boss giving her a stern stare before she went off with our orders and the promise of a signed picture from Marcus. He'd put her address in his phone.

"Will you really send her a picture?" I whispered.

"Of course. I told you, I don't tell lies. My Mother is a stickler for the truth." He didn't sound upset, so I didn't worry that I might have said something to piss him off.

The meal was surprisingly fast and tasty, but by the time we were stood on the pavement waving Nanna and Rachel off, it was late afternoon. I shuffled from one foot to the other. "I'd invite you back to the house, but my room is a shoe box and hardly big enough for me."

Marcus slung his arm around my shoulders as we walked back to the car. "It's cool. I've got to head back to London. I rejigged my schedule yesterday to come to get you, so I've a ton of work left to do this evening."

"Oh, I'm sorry."

His brows rose. "Why are you sorry? I'm not. I've had a wonderful time." At the car, he turned to face me, his arms tugging me into his body. "I've a jam-packed week, but I've a meeting down here with Sigrid and Griffin planned for Thursday evening. Do you want to go out for a late supper after I'm done?"

"Yeah, it's my turn to treat you."

The laughter lines deepened around his eyes and mouth. "Then I hope you've got enough to buy me a chippy dinner?"

My eyes widened. "You want fish and chips?"

"Hell yeah! Have you tried the ones from Fry Time?" I shook my head. "Then you're in for a treat." His lips brushed over mine. "They're almost as tasty as you." As if to prove how tasty I was, he groaned, deepening the kiss until my whole focus was his mouth touching mine.

Breathless and more than a little giddy when he let me go, I stared at him, hoping I wasn't looking as spaced as I felt. "You have a wonderful mouth."

Those same lips formed into a huge grin. He swooped in and gave me a hard kiss before stepping back. "You are far too tempting."

Something deep inside my chest clenched tight. "Is that a problem?"

"Nope, not one little bit."

A slow smile spread over my face. What a great answer.

CHAPTER FIFTEEN

Marcus

The phone in my back pocket rang, causing me to curse under my breath as I worked to keep my concentration on the male model who was currently holding an uncomfortable pose. The guys back muscles flexed and rippled under the strain of the heavy weights he held. "John, move your right arm a fraction to the left and tighten your triceps."

He did as I asked. "Okay, hold that." His skin glistened with sweat and the oil that I'd got him to slather over the top of his naked torso. The angle of the lights cast reflections over his skin as I captured shots of this new pose. The black shorts he wore hung low over his hips and stuck to his arse like a second skin. The man clearly loved to work out.

The sounds in the background of clanging weights hitting metal, grunts, and shouts were blocked out as I kept my camera trained on the man in front of me. I moved around him, capturing some of the clients using the gym in the background. Ronny, the owner of the gym, had got them all to sign a waiver for the use of the pictures before I'd started. I was a member of this gym and used it when I was home and had the time or inclination to work out. Ronny had wanted some professional images to help promote the new gyms he was opening across the southeast. It was a favour for a friend and why I was here late on a Tuesday evening, instead of at home chilling and having one of those random conversations with Fin. Since I'd dropped him home Sunday, we'd messaged back and forth, which made for some interesting threads of conversations.

The phone continued to ring in my back pocket. "Fuck sake." I lowered my camera and placed it on the stand Ronny had set up for me. "You can take five, John."

"Thank fuck," he muttered as the weights clanged against the stand sat off to the side. His free hands went up to the tops of his arms and rubbed at what were probably some very tired muscles.

I chuckled as I dug into my back pocket for my phone. Those who thought modelling was easy clearly hadn't tried it. It was anything but easy for the models.

Griffin's name flashed over the screen, and I rolled my eyes, now getting why it hadn't stopped ringing. "You know some of us to have to work for a living," I answered without preamble.

"And your point is?" he growled low and deep, the Scottish accent hardly noticeable.

"I'm working, and you won't quit ringing me." There was no heat, and Griffin's response was a grunt.

"I know if I don't keep ringing, you won't remember to check your phone when you've finished what you are doing. Which means it could be three days before you see a message. I've learnt my lesson, and now I have your attention. The meeting with Sigrid on Thursday, can you come to my place for it? Also, I'm having to move it to seven-thirty as I won't get back in the country until five, so it's all going to be a bit of a rush?"

"Shit, I've a date with Fin."

"Is that going to be a problem to cancel?" Griffin questioned.

My pulse kicked up a fuss at the very idea of cancelling. It had been only two days since I'd seen him, but I missed him. "It's a date. What would Charlie be like if you had to cancel?"

Griffin sighed, and my lips twitched. Since he'd gone all gay for Charlie, the man had turned into a big softie. "Bring him along. I'll organise food for everyone. But be warned, that probably means Nanna will want to join us."

"I had lunch with her on Sunday. Did she mention she took Fin underwear shopping?"

His laughter was instant. "She hasn't mentioned it, but then I've hardly had five minutes at home. Underwear shopping? Dear gods, the poor guy!"

"You have met Fin, I think he's an equal match for Agnes, so I wouldn't worry."

He made a noise that indicated he thought I was being stupid. "No one can handle Agnes, don't you be fooled."

It was my turn to laugh. "Is she giving you a rough time?"

"The woman is a menace and has a way of getting you to do things you never intended to do. If Alexander had met her years ago, I'm sure he'd have hired her. She's a shark dressed up in old lady clothes."

My laughter increased, causing several heads to turn in my direction. Alexander had been a kind of surrogate father to Griffin, as far as I could tell. When he'd died, he'd left him his whole hotel empire. I'd only met Alexander twice, through my mother's business dealing with him, but I'd liked his straightforward approach to things and his no-bullshit rule. "I'm sure he would have."

Griffin went back to the reason for the call. "So Thursday, is that a yes?"

"I'll speak to Fin, check with him, and let you know later tonight."

There was a moment of hesitation I didn't miss. "It sounds serious between you both?"

I rubbed at my chin, considering my answer. Griffin was a friend. "It's still early days, but yeah, I like him more than anyone I've dated before. He's different, and it seems I like that more than I expected." I shrugged while I walked back to my camera.

There was a shout in the background, and a muffling sound like Griffin had covered the mouthpiece of the phone. The muffled noises that followed sounded decidedly sexy. "Later."

I clicked off the phone and shook my head. I was sure that Griffin wouldn't even notice I'd gone while he had his tongue down his boyfriend's throat.

A worm of unpleasant jealousy slid greasily around my guts at not being able to kiss my own boyfriend any time I wanted. *Is he your boyfriend?*

Did a couple of dates constitute a relationship in Fin's eyes?

"We starting again?" John's question sank past the layer of worry.

I narrowed my gaze on the phone I still held. "Give me another five. I need to make one quick call." I didn't wait for John to respond as I walked off to a quieter part of the large gym, wanting a little privacy. I leant back against the mirrored wall and dialled Fin.

It rang for what felt like a long time before Fin finally answered. "Hello."

"Hey, Fin—"

"I thought you were working tonight? Isn't that what you said? Did I get mixed up? I'm on a study date."

A study date, what did he mean by that? "Who are you with?" I asked, keeping my tone light, which was hard when my innards were suddenly pushing their way up my body, trying to lodge themselves in my throat.

"Pippa."

A breath rushed out that I'd not noticed I'd been holding. "Say hi for me. I'm sorry to interrupt. Griffin has to change the time of our meeting on Thursday to seven-thirty."

"Oh, you're cancelling."

Did he sound disappointed? "No, no, I'm not cancelling, I'm ringing to see if you're happy to go to Griffin's so I don't have to change our plans. He's going to organise food, though he did warn me that Agnes will probably be there too." Did I sound lame? It sure as hell sounded like it to me.

"You're not cancelling, just combining your meeting with our date?"

When he put it like that, it didn't sound great. "Yeah, is that an issue?"

"Why would it be? You're taking me to an important meeting that means you're serious about me."

The way he laid it out got a big arse grin spreading over my face. "You wanna be my boyfriend?"

"I thought I was."

I laughed. "Yes, you are. I'm just being a dork."

"That's a change from me." There was a girlish giggle in the background, and Fin sighed. "I've gotta go. Pippa is being silly."

Minutes later, with the arrangements made to collect Fin on Thursday, I walked back to John, who looked a little bored just watching the other men training around us. "Let's get back to it."

"Someone put a big grin on your face."

"My boyfriend, Finlo," I answered, liking the way it sounded.

"Is he a model? Anyone I know?" John was someone I'd worked with once or twice before, and he was a friendly sort but a bit of a gossip. In the main, models were catty bitches.

"Nope, a history student." I grabbed my camera and changed the subject back to why we were there. "Right, can you use the twenty-kilo hand weights and do some lateral flies for me?"

Two days later, I pulled up outside Fin's home, and as planned, he was standing on the curb. Today he was dressed in his normal attire of ripped, baggy jeans and washed out T-shirt. Once more, he'd put on the Doc Martin's. Wasn't he roasting in those boots? It was warm this time of year, and boots seemed a little excessive. Was it a fashion statement? I discarded that thought as Fin was the least fashion-conscious person I knew.

The second I double-parked, he ran around the front of the car and quickly got into the passenger seat. I leant towards him and puckered my lips, which got a laugh. He hesitated, then pressed his lips softly to mine. What was meant to be a quick kiss was not. The taste of him was too tempting, as was the gentle exploration of his lips and tongue.

Unsure how long we kissed, it was the sound of a horn that finally got my head lifting. His pupils were huge, and his face was flushed, tempting me to go back to kissing him. He was draped over my lap, making it more than obvious how his kiss had affected me. I sucked in a shaky breath and encouraged him back into his own seat. Fuck, he was far too enticing.

His hands trembled while he buckled up. He didn't say a word.

Nerves danced over my skin. For want of anything better to do, I waved in apology to the car behind us, then drove off down the road.

The silence continued. I'd started to understand that when Fin went quiet, it was because he was usually thinking about his words carefully. Glancing sideways out the corner of my eye, I asked, "Is everything okay?"

"I missed you."

Wow.

The emotion in his voice was powerful and left me speechless at how much it struck at my burgeoning feelings for this wonderful man.

CHAPTER SIXTEEN

Finlo

I kept my hands in my lap, fighting the urge to slap my forehead. Why had I said that? I've never missed anyone before, but everything was different with Marcus. I'd tried to think about it all rationally, then I'd talked to Pippa. She'd not been rational at all with her 'pounce on Marcus and don't let go' advice. That left my mother, and though she could often give good advice, I wasn't sure Marcus being forced to meet her, as a result, was a good thing either.

Marcus remained silent for what felt like an eternity. Had I fucked up? Was I too needy? It sounded needy. "Sorry."

The man sat next to me, glanced sideways, his brows drawn together. "What are you sorry about?"

"For sounding needy. Or maybe for putting pressure on you. Is saying you miss someone deemed as needy? I've never said it before, so I'm not sure if it constitutes neediness." My hands were up in my hair, tugging, while Marcus indicated and pulled over. "What, why are we stopping? Do you want me to get out of the car?" For some reason, my heart sank at the idea of him asking me to get out. "What's wrong with me?"

Marcus undid his seatbelt and reached over the seat, taking hold of my hands. "Look at me." I couldn't resist. "There is nothing wrong with you. There is nothing wrong with saying you miss me. I like that you miss me. It doesn't make me feel stupid to say that I miss you too when we're not together." He placed my hands in my lap before he ran a fingertip down the side of my face, his eyes never wavering from mine. "Fin, where do you see this relationship going?"

"We're boyfriends." Was that the correct answer?

He chuckled. "That we are. What does that mean to you?"

I rubbed at my eyebrow, doing my best to keep eye contact. Was this some sort of test? "Are you testing me?"

The humour disappeared from his expression as he cupped my cheeks. "No, I'm not testing you. What I'm trying to figure out is what all this means to you. You're so literal at times. I just want to figure out if we are on the same page. The emotion you portrayed in what you said, I...liked it...a lot."

"Oh. You could hear that? I like you a lot too. Does that make us on the same page? I'm never normally on any page because, by the time I get to the book, everyone else has finished."

Marcus's smile was back, and the spark in his eyes was the only warning I got before he leant in and pressed his lips firmly against mine. The world got fuzzy, and my body reacted to the tongue stroking against mine. Marcus's mouth was...when he stopped kissing me, I'd maybe be able to think of something.

His ability to make the constant clutter in my mind seem to disappear was a talent that I was starting to...love? My pulse picked up, and I drew back, widening eyes meeting Marcus's. "My mind is very fuzzy. Do you think that's why it's thinking about the word 'love'?"

Marcus's breath hit my face in short bursts. The hands on my face trembled as emotions ran over his face, leaving me uncertain. Why did I always have to spill what was in my head out of my mouth? "I'm so—"

He pressed a finger to my lips. "Don't apologise for speaking the truth about your feelings." He sucked in a breath, and a look of what appeared to be uncertainty crossed his face. "The feelings I have for you are strong. Stronger than I've ever experienced with anyone I've ever dated. I'm not sure I'm ready to attach the L word to them though. Is it okay if we table this conversation for now?"

I nodded, my mouth too dry to speak, and with my brain, it was probably for the best that I stay quiet, or I'd spoil things by what would pour out of my lips. The soft kiss that followed settled my racing heart. His nose touched mine for the briefest of moments. "You are a special man."

Unsure what to say to that, I remained quiet.

Several minutes later, Marcus parked outside Griffin and Charlie's home. We'd hardly got out of the car when the door opened to reveal Nanna. "You're both late." She pointed and grinned. "Have you two been trying out the dogging thing again?"

"Nanna!" Charlie cried out, appearing from behind her.

"Dear gods stop her," Griffin growled as he followed after Charlie.

"How am I supposed to stop her?" Charlie asked.

Only, he didn't appear to be talking to anyone in particular as his gaze was moving between us all. Nanna shook her head, and the light in her eyes warned she wasn't finished having fun. "Did you know it's a popular pastime for a lot of people? After you took me to the nice bar where they have those lovely men who dress up as cute puppies, I went on the thingamabob. Did you know there are lots of things people like to do for—"

"Nanna, please stop now," Charlie begged, his eyes pleading as they moved from Nanna to Griffin. He didn't look like he was going to be much help when he visibly paled, whereas Marcus was shaking with silent laughter. What was a thingamabob? And was she talking about a sex club? I opened my mouth but didn't get the chance to say a word.

"Fucking feed me," came the now-familiar maniacal voice, just as Cissy appeared between Nanna's legs.

Marcus made a kind of choking noise. I patted his arm. "It's only Cissy. She gets a little tetchy when she's hungry." I bent down and stuck out my hand to the large tabby who was wandering towards us.

"The cat...talks?" Marcus didn't sound like his normal self.

I looked up at him, offering a reassuring smile. "Of course. I'm trying to teach my hamster to talk, but so far, he's not interested. Though that might be because it lives with my mum and she's not as patient as me. It might also be 'cause I've only visited twice in the last few months." I stood when Cissy decided to head back into the house.

There was an awkward silence, one I recognised as they often happened around me.

"You have a hamster?" Marcus asked, his face betraying nothing as he reached to take my hand.

"Yep. The tepee Mum lives in is big but not that big, so I couldn't have anything that would take up too much room."

"A tepee," Charlie, Griffin and Marcus said at the same time.

"Why yes, a tepee." I smiled at all three men. "She has a small bit of land, and she didn't want to have anything that impacted on the environment, so she chose a tepee."

"He's invited us to go visit with his mum, isn't that right, laddie?" Nanna came and took hold of my arm. "Come on, I've a few things I want you to see while the boys talk business." Marcus looked amused as I shrugged and let Nanna guide me past the other men.

"Nanna, what's a thingamabob?"

She giggled. "You know, the thing you can use to search and find all kinds of interesting things on. Did you know that Charlie and Griffin like BSMD?"

There was a strangled cry behind us, right before Charlie shouted out, "It's BDSM, and we don't like it, Nanna. Please, if you love me, stop talking about sex stuff."

We came to a stop halfway down the hall, and she gave me a sly wink before looking back over her shoulder. "Charlie, of course, I love you. You don't need to be ashamed that you and Grif are kinky."

She didn't give them a chance to say a word as she carried on down the hallway that led to her part of the house. There was the sound of several muttered curses as the door closed behind us.

Seconds later, we were in her large lounge room. The grin she gave me was impish. "You have to keep them on their toes, laddie. Boring is for when you're in a coffin ten feet under the ground."

What was there to say to that?

Rachael appeared from the kitchen, a wide smile on her homely face. The flowing kaftan she wore was in bright cerise. "There you are. I wondered where you'd got to."

Nanna matched Rachael's smile. "I went to find Fin. What did you do with the bag of goodies?"

"It's over there by the window, at the side of the sofa. I put it there so Charlie wouldn't spy it." Her hands clapped together as a sparkle of what appeared to be excitement lit her eyes.

Why wouldn't they want Charlie to see the bag? I got a sinking feeling when Nanna retrieved the bag and waved it at me. "We were in a rush the other night when we went to get new underwear, and I forgot about Sigrid's fancy underwear. Then it was like kismet that Griffin mentioned Sigrid was coming tonight for their meeting. Did you know he's launching a range of lingerie for men? She did some amazing designs, so I asked her if I could have some. She's such a lovely lady, as is her girlfriend. You'll get to meet her tonight. She's coming to dinner too."

Nanna carried on talking, but I wasn't sure what about as I'd got stuck on lingerie. Wasn't that something that women wore? She wasn't expecting me to try some on, or was she going to? The sinking feeling increased when the bag was upended, and the contents spilt out onto the sofa. An array of pretty, pastel-coloured underwear covered the sofa, all of it looking far too flimsy to wear.

They were way too small for Nanna, which could only mean one thing. Wide-eyed, I glanced from the sofa to Nanna. "Erm…what…why…no." It was the best I could come up with.

"Don't be silly. They're all in your size. I made sure of that."

The gleam in her eye left me sweaty. She picked up a pale pink pair of silk and lace panties. My heart started to thump unpleasantly against my chest. "No. Honestly, I don't need these."

"Of course you do. You'll look fabulous in them. Charlie does," she tagged on as if that was going to make me feel any better.

"Charlie is gorgeous, and a sought after model. I'm none of those things."

You are to Marcus.

The second that thought popped into my head, I stared at the underwear, recalling why we were here tonight. Had Marcus seen Charlie in underwear like this? Something unfamiliar unfurled inside my guts. Was I jealous?

Nanna didn't give me time to think beyond that thought. "Strip. Let's see if they fit."

I held up my hands, even knowing it was useless to fight against the light of determination I could see when Nanna closed the distance between us.

My protests fell on deaf ears, or that's how it seemed when I somehow found myself in Nanna's bedroom, changing into the pink panties. The silk touching my skin was…a revelation. Was this why women liked to wear silk?

"Laddie, you decent?"

Here goes nothing. "I'm coming."

A full-body flush coated my skin when I stepped into Nanna's lounge room, trying not to squirm at the scrutiny of both women.

"They're a good fit. See, I was right. The pale colours really suit his milky skin."

"Agnes—"

I froze, as did the man who'd just stepped into the room. His eyes roamed down my body in a heated look I'd seen before. My body started to respond.

"You look hot," Nanna said.

"That's embarrassment. I'm not hot, really just flushed from..." I'm aroused, I'm aroused in front of two women...my hands dropped to my groin, and I took a step backwards.

Marcus walked over to me, blocking me from Nanna and Rachael. "You look gorgeous." His gaze dropped, the desire making the situation in my underwear all the more obvious. "I think it's best you go get dressed, but leave those on," he said, loud enough for only me to hear.

"Really?" I squeaked.

A wolfish grin appeared on Marcus's face. "Really."

CHAPTER SEVENTEEN

Marcus

The photos I was supposed to be reviewing for selection failed to hold my attention, and I cursed Agnes. The woman was a menace, and the bag of underwear she'd given Fin had been playing on my mind. I'd had no further chance to see Fin in the pretty underwear as the meeting and meal had gone on late into the night. I had an early start the following day, so once it was finally time to leave, all we'd managed was a couple of heated kisses in the car. Since then, my over-full diary had prevented me from squeezing in a trip to Brighton.

It was Sunday morning, and I was due at a photoshoot in two hours. I'd not been able to sleep, with thoughts of Fin running through my mind, so I'd got out of bed to come down to work.

How's that going for you?

The sigh was loud in the quiet of my studio. For years, I'd worked full throttle, packing my days with adventure and excitement, keeping myself too busy to notice there was something missing from my life. Why hadn't I stopped to find a partner before now? I'm thirty-six. Still young, I suppose, but I'd never had a serious relationship up to now. Why was that?

I'd no real answer. Did that make me sad or selfish?

I reached from my mobile and dialled my mother.

"Marcus, you're up with the larks this morning. To what do I owe the pleasure of a call?"

I grinned. "That's not a hint of sarcasm, is it?"

"Why, I don't know what you mean. I've left several messages with Steve, but you've been avoiding me since you set me up on a…date with Jed!"

"I did no such thing. I merely booked a table, then work got in the way, and Jed kindly stepped in to keep you company." I heard a very unladylike snort and laughed. "Mum, you need to start living again. You're attractive, and when you let go, you're fun to be around. I want you to be happy."

"I am happy," she argued, but there was no heat in her voice, only...sadness.

"Are you really? You're holed up in your office eighty percent of the time. When was the last time you had a holiday?"

"When was the last time *you* had a holiday?" she fired back.

My smile dipped. I was my mother's son. "We're a pair, aren't we?"

"I suppose we are," she replied, sounding resigned.

My heart pounded painfully. "I've met someone, and I like him... more than anyone I've ever dated before."

"You've never introduced me to anyone you've dated in the past, so I'm going to be no help there. Am I going to get to meet..."

"Finlo, and yes, I'd like you to meet him. He's special, Mum." I ran a hand through my hair and got up to wander over to the back wall and the array of photos that hung there. I ran a finger over the edge of the picture of Fin smiling at Nanna while she talked. He'd given her his full attention, which was something I noticed he didn't often do. He'd paid me the same attention, and it left me feeling...important.

I exhaled a shaky breath.

"It sounds like you've a wealth of feelings for this man."

"I do. I think I'm in... love with him. Fuck, isn't it too soon? We've only had a handful of dates."

Warm laughter came down the speaker. "Son, you can't put a measure of time on love. Sometimes all it takes is one look, and you know. For others, it takes time to build the foundation. Bring him to dinner this week."

"I'll see when he's free to come to London. Promise me you won't scare him off."

"If he's scared off by me, then he's not any kind of man for my son." There was indignation and, if I wasn't mistaken, humour in her voice.

"You're a scary person...just ask Jed."

"Stop right there. We are not talking about Jed. We're talking about you."

"We were, now we're back on the subject of Jed. Invite him to dinner too, and we'll double date." I kept the laughter out of my voice.

"Dear Gods, have you lost your mind. I'm not double dating with my son."

"Give over, of course, you are. I'll let you know which night we can come and say hi to Jed for me." I ended the call before she could say another word. I switched off my phone, knowing she'd ring me straight back. She hated not getting in the last word. I was the same. Laughing and feeling lighter after the call, I finished what I'd been doing before grabbing my camera bag to head out. I needed to work on how I might get a little more time with Fin to figure out the depth of my feelings.

"You never said where abouts we were heading in London, to visit your mum," Fin said, looking at me as I took the road leading to the motorway.

"I didn't? I was sure I mentioned where the house was?" I hadn't, and I didn't sound all that convincing. *Bugger it.* I kept facing forward, not needing to see Fin's face when he spoke and confirmed that I'd been rumbled.

"No, you didn't. Are you ambushing me? Is that what it's called when you take someone somewhere without letting them know where they are going?"

I chuckled. "Would you be pissed if I said yes?" When I chanced a glance in his direction, his brows were doing their best to merge in the middle of his forehead. "My mum lives in an exclusive part of London."

"Are you embarrassed?" Fin questioned.

I dialled back the humour, but it was hard when Fin looked so damn adorable at calling me out. "Maybe."

"It's all right. I'll not judge you." His hand appeared, holding his phone. "Now it's official that we're at the stage of meeting mums. You'll need to meet mine. She's been nagging me ever since I first mentioned I had a boyfriend."

"I've no issue with that." And I didn't. From all I'd heard about Fin's mum, she was an *interesting* person.

"You say that now. You wait."

There was no point in arguing about it, but a sliver of unease curled its way around the pit of my stomach. "Your mum will love me. Everyone does."

He snorted. "If you were a tree, maybe."

A tree?

His phone beeped a few seconds later. "Are you free on Sunday? I forgot Nanna and Racheal are heading up to my mum's then. You could tag along too. That way, you won't have to deal with her all on your own. Sometimes more is better when meeting Mum for the first time."

The seriousness of his tone increased the feeling in my gut. "I'll make Sunday work."

"Great. I'll give you the directions."

The conversation switched to Fin's course after that. He only had a few months left till he'd obtain his masters. "Have you come up with any ideas about what you want to do when you leave uni?"

"Seriously, no. I've been looking around, and there isn't much call for a history major that isn't interested in teaching."

The glum expression he wore was hard to resist. I laid a hand on his thigh, and he covered it with one of his. "I'm sure it will all work out."

"Let's hope. The last thing I want to do is go back to living with Mum. I've got used to having a bathroom with a shower in it."

No bathroom? That opened up all kinds of questions. "Doesn't your mum have a bathroom?"

"It's a tepee. There's no place to put a bathroom inside it," he answered in all seriousness.

"How long has she lived in the tepee?"

"I'm twenty-four, and I think she said she bought it the year before she found out she was pregnant. Maybe twenty-six years? She'd been squatting on the land for I don't know how long before that. Did you know that years ago, if you lived on unclaimed land for fifteen years or more, the land title could be claimed by the squatter? It's how Mum got the land she lives on. I think the laws have been changed since, possibly because of her."

My brows shot up my forehead as I glanced from the busy motorway to Fin. I wasn't sure what information to process first. "Your childhood home was a tepee?"

"Why yes, where else would I have lived? I told you she lived in a tepee last week?"

I squeezed his leg. "Sorry, I was just a little surprised. What was it like growing up in a tepee?"

He shrugged. "Same as living anywhere only without indoor plumbing. Oh, and proper heat, with no kitchen. Although I suppose the small stove could be classified as a kitchen and heater. It would have been classed as such in Neolithic times."

He carried on comparing the way he was raised to similarities between his home and what cavemen had centuries ago. It was so fascinating how his mind worked that before I realised it, we'd hit London and were nearly at my childhood home.

My earlier nervousness about the home I'd grown up in started to build again, and my fingers tapped on the steering wheel as we stopped at a set of traffic lights.

Would Fin freak out at the opulence of the home I grew up in?

CHAPTER EIGHTEEN

Fin

What I'd pictured in my head would be Marcus's mother's home, didn't even come close to the…I wasn't sure what the correct term would be for the large building I could see. Mansion? There was an electronic gate guarding the drive, leading up to the massive stone house that had to be three storeys and looked more like four homes stuck together than one.

"This is where you grew up?"

Marcus didn't answer straight away. He drove up the drive and parked by the large red door with a big brass knocker on the front of it. "Yeah, my father bought it back in the sixties when house prices in London weren't astronomical."

He didn't look at me. Was he nervous? I eyed the way his fingers continued to tap at the steering wheel. "Are you nervous?"

That got his head to turn in my direction. "A little, if I'm honest. Money isn't something I think about often. Listening to you," he pointed to the large house, "and how you grew up, it's hugely different to me."

"How is it different, other than this is a brick building?. You were loved? Clothed? Fed? I was the same. Where that happens is irrelevant, is it not?" Was I being too simplistic? Pippa and some of my tutors often said I was.

A smile spread slowly over his face, and he leant in, making my heart skip merrily along at what was coming next. It had been five days since he'd kissed me, and the brief touch of lips when I'd got in the car earlier did not count as a kiss. "I keep saying it, but I can't help it. You're very special," he whispered against my lips.

The kiss that followed was everything I'd come to expect, only with one difference. This one held something intangible I couldn't explain. It managed to captivate my heart in the gentleness of the caress, and I didn't want it to stop. His mouth moved slowly over mine, lips soft, exploring as if he was trying to learn every dip and curve.

Mine parted, and his tongue dipped between my lips into my mouth. I groaned and wrapped my arms around his neck. My body warmed. Sensations flooded my chest, and I clung on, never wanting the moment to end.

Marcus released me, leaving me fuzzy eyed and feeling way too warm.

"Right this minute, I'm regretting agreeing to dinner. I want to take you home and—"

"Please don't say it. I won't be able to meet your mum and act normal. Okay, that is never going to be possible. I mean, what's normal? It's not something that's really quantifiable, is it? Maybe I meant decent? My body, this second, is anything but that, and it really won't be good to go into the house with," I squirmed in my seat as Marcus's grin became wicked, "well, you know what." I shut my eyes and moved back. "Stop looking at me like that."

He laughed. "Like what?"

I shook my head and opened my eyes to look at the unrepentant man next to me. "You're as bad as Nanna. Full of mischief."

"I'm taking that as a compliment. Let's go in so we can leave."

"You sound like me," I said as I opened the door.

"It's great," he answered before getting out of the car.

A grin spread over my face. Did he mean that?

There was no chance to think about it further as Marcus all but dragged me into his childhood home. The inside was warm and welcoming, even with its sleek, modern lines, which were nothing like the architecture of the exterior.

I stopped to look when Marcus shouted out, "Mum, where are you?"

A woman I'd met briefly at the fashion show appeared from a room off to the left. Dressed in an elegant khaki trouser suit, with not a hair out of place. Her expression gave little away, though her eyes were assessing as they looked me up and down. "Do you always need to shout?"

There was an impatient bite to her words, but Marcus didn't seem to notice, or if he did, he ignored it. "This place is huge. Shouting is a necessity."

"For you, yes."

A man appeared behind her, similarly dressed in a navy suit. "Marcus."

"Jed, good to see you." Marcus guided us closer to the couple. "This is Fin, my *boyfriend*."

Why was he stressing the last part?

I frowned as we stopped in front of the couple, who were still standing in the doorway.

Jed offered his hand. "Nice to meet you, Fin."

Shaking the hand, I smiled politely. "Same, my name is Finlo, really, but only my mum calls me that. But not all the time."

Marcus wrapped his arm around my waist, and I glanced at him. Was I waffling? Of course, I was. "Sorry."

"You've nothing to be sorry for," Marcus said as he lowered his head and his mouth pressed softly to mine. "Relax," he whispered against my mouth.

There was a discreet cough, and Marcus sighed, then straightened but kept his arm around me. "The woman making the discreet coughing noise is my mum, Wendy."

Wendy's expression didn't change, her face a smooth mask.

"What's for dinner, Mum?"

"I've had the chef prepare your favourite." She glanced at me. "Fin, do you have any allergies or food dislikes I need to advise the chef of?"

"Oh, shouldn't you have asked me about this before? The poor chef has probably already made the meal for everyone? It's not good to waste food. Thing is, I don't eat meat. I do, but I don't." I rubbed at my temple when it started to throb. "What I mean is I only eat it once a year. If you've had the chef make a meat dish, I'll eat it as I haven't had one so far this year," I offered helpfully.

Wendy blinked several times as her gaze moved from me to Marcus and back. Her expression was nigh on impossible to read, yet there was tension around her jawline, and her posture was stiff.

"My favourite is macaroni cheese," Marcus said, and I sagged against him, enjoying the warmth of his embrace.

I smiled at everyone. "I like mac cheese, crisis averted."

Marcus laughed, as did Jed, but Wendy's lips thinned. Did she dislike me? That was a real possibility.

Seconds later, we were led into a brightly lit room where a grey marble dining table was set for four people. The glasses and cutlery gleamed against the glittery surface. Marcus pulled out a leather and chrome chair, encouraging me to sit. Once in the chair, he whispered in my ear, "She's as stressed as you. I've never brought anyone home to meet her before. Just be you. She'll love you."

The fluttering that started in the centre of my chest at his confession spread through my body to the point I wasn't sure if I was going to be able to pick up my cutlery when my hands started to shake. There was that word again— love—only this time it felt more significant in these circumstances.

Marcus took my hand in his and laid them on the table. Wendy eyed our hands, then her gaze met mine. I offered her a friendly smile. "I'm nice."

There was a kind of choking noise coming from Marcus, and I was back to squirming. Why had I said that? Barely resisting smacking my forehead, I squeezed Marcus's hand in apology.

"I'm sure you are. Can you tell me a little about yourself, Fin?" Wendy asked, in a tone that I recognised as a demand, not a real question.

"Mum," Marcus growled.

One brow rose the merest of fractions. Had she done something to her face to make it not move? "What? You've brought a *young* man home to meet me for the first time. I want to get to know him."

Jed shifted in his seat, his lips quivering.

"Then stop with the whole intimidating boss act. He's my boyfriend, not a business acquaintance." The hand holding mine tightened.

"This is awkward," I muttered.

Marcus coughed, and Jed made a noise in the back of his throat that told me I'd been louder than I thought. I sighed.

"It's okay, your mum is worried. I'm not that young. I'm twenty-four. Though I suppose that could seem young next to everyone in the room." I shrugged at the chuckle Marcus didn't hide. "Is age important? I've never really thought about it. When I'm with Marcus, I don't think. I feel. He makes me see the world differently. Through his eyes, I've the ability to feel all the emotions he captures with his images. They give me an opportunity to live inside his mind, if only for a short while. It connects us in a way that goes beyond surface nonsense. Does any of that have anything to do with age? Maybe it does because he's lived longer and learnt more, I don't know."

Wendy's lips quivered, and there was a sheen to her eyes. "You're in love with my son," she said bluntly.

"I…well…I'm" I looked at Marcus, who was glaring across the table. Did I love him?

Suddenly the room temperature seemed to go up twenty degrees, and I tugged at the collar of the smartest T-shirt I owned. "I don't think we should be talking about feelings here. That's a conversation for me and Marcus, don't you think?" I asked with uncertainty. Should we talk about it in front of his mother? Would she like me more if I did?

"Mum, really, did you have to?" Marcus glanced back at me, his expression hard to read. "It's okay. We'll talk later." The sincerity of his words helped my wildly beating pulse but didn't unknot my stomach. His attention turned once again to his mother. "Are you quite finished making Fin feel uncomfortable?"

Her cheeks pinked, but I couldn't tell what she was thinking with her unmoving face. In the hopes of easing the crackling tension that had risen in the last few seconds, I spoke. "I'm at uni doing a masters in history. I'm not financially rich, but I'm not after your son's money. I wasn't actually aware he had any when we started dating, although I've no way of proving that." I looked down at my clothes. "I'm just me. I have debt and no job prospects right now, so I suppose that could seem suspicious to a mother who's worried for her child."

There was the kind of pregnant pause, the kind I'd never figured out if I should fill it or not.

I breathed a sigh of relief when, for the first time, Wendy smiled, though there wasn't so much as a line around her eyes or mouth. "Thank you for being honest."

"You're welcome."

Marcus squeezed my hand once more before he released it when a young girl appeared with a bottle of wine, which he took, then proceeded to pour it into the glasses.

"Are you ready to be served, ma'am?"

"Yes, Lidia, tell the chef to serve the first course."

After the first course arrived, things seemed a little more relaxed, although I wasn't totally sure because I'd never been in this kind of situation before. Marcus talked about several projects he was working on. Jed didn't say very much, but his gaze lingered a lot on Wendy, not that she seemed to notice.

I kept quiet.

When the main course was placed in front of me, I sniffed the warm, scented air. "This smells much nicer than the stuff you get in those ready-made packets I buy from the supermarket."

Marcus grinned at me. "Wait till you try it."

Jed ate a mouthful and groaned. "This is wonderful."

Wendy nodded, her face back to going pink as she met Jed's gaze. It held for what seemed to be an awfully long time.

"How long have you been dating?" I asked.

Jed choked on the next mouthful, and Wendy's eyes widened, though her forehead remained smooth. "Jed is my assistant."

"Okay. I'm not sure what that has to do with dating?" My fork hovered in the air as I tilted my head to scrutinise the pair in front of me. "It's obvious there is something more between you both. Is it that you don't talk about it because you work together? I suppose people might judge the level of professionalism between you. Mum always said life is wasted by worrying about what others think. You can't stop it or change it, so why waste your life worrying about it?"

Marcus's shoulders started to shake, and I glanced at him. Evidently, he was struggling to keep his laughter in. His eyes danced with humour. "You're perfect."

"Why? I don't understand." I placed my fork down.

"These two have been avoiding the obvious attraction they feel for each other for years." He leant over and pressed a kiss to my lips. "You summed it up brilliantly, having only just met them. As I said, perfect."

I wasn't sure if the night was a success or not by the time we left, two hours later. Wendy had loosened up some and had smiled a total of four times. Jed was a little more reserved, whereas I'd made up for that by being myself and saying whatever came into my head.

There was the heady scent of flowers as we stood on the doorstep, readying to leave. "Thank you for dinner."

"You're welcome. It was nice to meet you, Fin."

Realising that she sounded like she meant it, my lips pulled into a grin.

Marcus slung his arm over my shoulder and tugged me close to him. "I'll ring you next week, Mum." He moved, taking me with him to kiss his mother's cheek. She smelt of expensive perfume. Was I supposed to kiss her cheek too?

"Make sure you do," Wendy answered and moved back, making the decision easier for me.

A chuckle followed as Marcus gave her a one-arm salute. A minute later, we were back in the car and heading down the drive.

"That went well."

I glanced at Marcus, unable to make out his expression in the shadowed interior. "Are you sure?"

"I am, and do you know why?"

My heart skipped a beat. "No."

The car idled at the end of the drive, waiting for the electronic gate to open. Marcus glanced at me with an intensity that fizzed in the confines of the car, causing my skin to buzz. "Because you're you, and you don't try to be something you're not."

Oh my!

CHAPTER NINETEEN

Marcus

The tension in Fin's body disappeared, and the sexy smile that followed left me hitting the accelerator the second the gates opened. The need to get him back to my home so I could do all the things I'd thought about over the last few days was like an itch I couldn't scratch fast enough.

Fin remained silent, the sexual tension between us building as he stroked his hand up and down my thigh for the remaining drive. My cock bucked each and every time his fingers grazed the top of my thigh. If it had been anyone else but Fin, I'd have thought the move was planned to make me edgy and desperate, but the man didn't have a contrived bone in his body.

Breathing through my teeth, and with great difficulty, I focused on the road, counting down the minutes. Painfully hard by the time I got out of the car at my home, I all but dragged Fin up the path, though he didn't seem to mind, judging by the way he was grinning.

Through the door, I'd barely clicked the lock in place before I pounced. The previous days had felt like an eternity, and now I wanted him naked. Fin's mouth was as eager as mine when our lips met. The urgency continued as my hands tugged at his clothes, my mouth not wanting to release his. The wine he'd drunk sweetened his mouth, yet there was still the unique taste of my man.

I swallowed his moan as our tongues slid against each other. Pushing up his T-shirt, my fingers skimmed over his bare skin, gaining a whimper. "I want you naked."

"Underwear," he replied breathlessly.

My head lifted. Fin's eyes were unfocused, his lips swollen. "Underwear?" I asked in confusion. What had I missed?

"Nanna's underwear," he said as if that explained it.

I blinked and took a deep breath, though it didn't get a chance to sit in my lungs for more than a second before it rushed right back out when I realised what he meant. Swallowing, my gaze lowered to his jeans. "Do you have something pretty on under there?" I rasped.

"I'm not sure it's pretty." A blush rose up his neck and flooded his face, and his hands fluttered at his sides.

"Upstairs, now! We are not doing this in the hallway." I ran a hand through my hair and hesitated. A question popped into my mind and out of my mouth. "Would you let me photograph you?"

Fin's body jerked. "Oh no, why...no...really...I don't..."

"Fin, take a breath." Only once he'd done it twice did I speak again, unsure what I was going to say until I opened my mouth. "I love you. I love your body. I love your uniqueness. To me, you are beautiful in every way."

"Holy fuck!" He held up his hands, then immediately dropped them. "We're talking about love, aren't we? Like, the real kind that involves the heart and not the head. Though I suppose your head is involved too 'cause you have to think about stuff." He shook his head as if trying to clear it. "I wasn't sure when your mum brought up the love word earlier, it was going to be now we'd have this conversation. I don't know why though, I mean, we're alone, and it seems like the logical time. Only I was kind of hoping for the naked part now, too just to be clear, but if you want to talk, that's all right—"

Seeing he was going to keep going, I took hold of his hands. "Fin."

"I'm waffling, aren't I?"

I nodded. "A little, it's okay. It wasn't my plan to blurt it out like that either, but there is nothing about us that follows any rhythm or reason, and for me, that works. I didn't say the words to put pressure on you. It just felt right to say them."

He started to shake, then he was in my arms and his mouth seeking mine. The kiss was demanding and sexily hot in that it left me pushing him back against the wall to cage him in. Any thoughts of continuing the conversation fled. One hand hooked under his left leg, lifting it to hook it around my hip, allowing our groins to meet. His solid arousal pressed against mine, and we groaned together.

The kiss continued, wet and so damn dirty. His hands seemed to be everywhere as his hips rocked forward. Arousal met arousal, and it was hard to remember my own name, never mind that this wasn't what I'd had in mind.

His hand cupped my arse and squeezed hard, forcing my cock to push against his. "Naked, I need you naked."

"That," he gasped against my wet lips.

I sucked in a shaky breath and did the one thing I didn't want to do. I dropped his leg and took a step back, then another. Chest heaving, I eyed the man leaning on the wall, all sexily dishevelled. My hands itched for my camera. I wanted him to see what I could. "Please let me photograph you."

Heavy-lidded eyes stared at me for the longest time before he nodded in a measured way he didn't often do, so I got how significant this was to him.

I exhaled noisily. "These pictures are for us and no one else, I promise. Go up to my bedroom, I'll be up in a minute."

Wordlessly, he walked to the stairs. I took a few breaths to help with the hammering heart doing its best to escape my chest. After he disappeared from sight, I went down to my studio to grab my Canon SX740. It was small and perfect for what I had in mind.

Fin had used his time wisely. On entering my bedroom a minute later, my heart leapt into my throat at the man in the centre of my bed. Fingers tightened on my camera while my gaze travelled down the semi-naked man who'd captured my heart with his quirkiness.

The turquoise silk panties, trimmed in white lace, were high waisted and cut high over the top of the hip bones. His slim hips were accentuated by the cut of the silk and trim of the lace. Milky white skin glowed in the light of the lamps he'd switched on. The stark contrast of his skin against the colour of the panties and the navy cover he lay on left me aching with desire. "You look spectacular."

My camera was up and to my eye before I'd registered my own intention. He was breathtakingly beautiful whether he could see it or not. My camera captured image after image to show him how wrong he was about himself. His expression, one I hoped I'd get to see every damn day, was open, and his heart was there for me to see, to treasure.

I'd no clue how long I spent moving around the bed immortalising him. His cock remained hard and pressing against the silk. His chest rose and fell in quick succession, but he didn't move or hide from me. He offered me a priceless gift I'd never forget: his trust.

There was a damp patch at the front of his panties by the time I knelt, naked with a cloaked cock, on the bed and bent to kiss him. His lips parted, and he moaned into my mouth. Capturing each sound, I licked at his lips. He lay plaint on the bed, leaving me to lead. I kissed my way to his ear and down the slim column of his neck. He shivered, his hands clenching into the cover.

"Beautiful," I murmured as my lips tasted his warm skin. I kissed my way over his collarbone and down to his well-defined pectoral muscles. He groaned as I sucked the tip of his budded nipple into my mouth. He was all long lines and angles, his skin as smooth as the silk of the panties he wore.

"I love how smooth you are."

His answer was to tremble with each stroke of my tongue as it licked a path from his concave belly to the top of the lace. At the edge of the lace, he gasped and wiggled on the cover, his hips lifting invitingly. I nibbled my way over the damp silk, pushing my nose into it to inhale his musky scent.

"Smell so damn delicious." I licked at the silk, and the faint taste of precum left me hungry for more.

On and on, I explored him, kissing down one long, slim leg and working my way back up the other, worshipping his body until he was making a constant stream of noises. By the time I slipped the panties down his legs, his skin was flushed with desire and his heavy-lidded eyes were begging me for more.

Kneeling between his thighs, I opened the lube bottle I'd tucked under the pillow earlier. Keeping my eyes locked on Fin's, I poured a liberal amount over his cock and balls. His lips parted, and he gasped. "Chilly."

I chuckled. "Not for long."

Capping the bottle, I threw it to the other side of the bed and ran a finger over his erection, making it pulse and a pearl of precum bead at the tip. Leaning in, I swirled my tongue over the tip as I slowly slid my fingers down his hot erection, teasing the flesh and gathering the lube. His thighs shook as I cupped his balls while continuing to slide my tongue over the head of his cock, tasting his essence. I tortured us both before I circled his pucker and pushed the tip of a finger in, past the tight rim of muscle.

His arse clenched down hard, and he arched, pushed down, and moaned. "Like that."

His voice was a sexy rasp. I ignored the ache going on between my thighs. This was all about pleasing Fin. I'd wanted to take my time, tease us both, but it seemed Fin had other ideas. His hips thrust up to push my finger deeper. With a cry, he rocked back then forward again, seeking his own pleasure. His lips parted, desire swirling in the depths of his eyes as they held mine. He continued to move fluidly back and forth as imagery of what it was going to feel like to be deep inside him filled my mind. My cock bucked when he clenched his hot, silky channel around my finger.

My jaw ached as I sank a second finger in with the first after his encouragement, then torment started again. As I sank into him, he clenched, withered, and moaned. We established a routine as I stretched him; sink in, clench, moan, relax. Sink in, clench, moan, relax. On and on, it went until my hair was stuck to my forehead, and my balls were painfully tight with need. So much so, I worried I'd embarrass myself the second I got inside him.

"Need you, please, I'm ready. I'm more than ready, Marcus. Please, fuck me," he begged and rocked on my three fingers as if to prove his point.

Gently removing my fingers, I moved to sit up and wipe the remaining lube over the condom. Breath hissed out between my teeth at the mere touch. I met his gaze. Fuck, I'd never felt this need before. How was a person supposed to survive this?

There was no obvious answer as I shifted over the stunning man that wanted to be mine. Our hips aligned, and my cock slid against his in a wet caress. He groaned, and his chest arched up, his lips parting as he gasped. "So good. Why has it never felt like this before?"

I captured his mouth in a blistering kiss and moved to press him into the cover so my cock could push against his slick arse. "'Cause this means something special. Bare down for me," I whispered against his mouth. Doing as I requested, the head of my cock pushed past the still tight rim of muscle.

Breathless and struggling not to go deep, I inched in slowly. The heat and feel of him wrapped around my cock was indescribable and something I never wanted to end. By the time I was nestled fully against him, hot puffs of air were brushing over my face.

Fin's eyelids had drooped to mere slits, his lips parted and slick from our kisses. In all my life, I'd never felt more connected to a person than I did at this moment. There was no space between us. Our hearts beat in unison as I slowly drew my hips back to push back into his tight sheath, trying to convey how precious he was to me. The urgent need warred with the desire to give this man everything he deserved. Time spiralled away from us. The world spun around the feelings that were building between us until all I could see, feel, know, was Fin.

I brushed my lips gently over his as his channel clenched down and his body shuddered against mine, wet heat spreading between us.

His glazed eyes held mine as he breathed out, "I love you."

The words stole the remainder of my breath. Uncontrollable tingling started at the base of my spine, and my balls tightened. My cock erupted seconds later. Pulse after pulse of cum filled the condom as I held Fin's gaze, hoping that he could see the truth and depth of what I felt for him. "God, I love you."

CHAPTER TWENTY

Fin

Nanna and Rachael talked over each other in the front of the car about the best route to take to my mum's place. I'd already given them directions, only they both didn't seem to want to follow them.

"Are you planning on taking me on a detour?" I asked as we missed the exit we were supposed to take, twenty minutes later. Sweat gathered on my top lip as I checked the time. Marcus, at this rate, was going to get to Mum's before we did. I'd warned him to be careful about what subjects he talked about, hadn't I?

Nanna twisted around in the passenger seat to look back at me. I'd a feeling she'd made a real effort with her appearance, though I'd no clue why. Where we were going was more fit for old clothes. Nanna's chic looking pink organza dress, which floated about her frame, matched the cute pair of low heeled cherry red shoes that were going to get wrecked. Had it rained in the last week? The land the tepee was on could get a little boggy when it rained heavily. "Life's one big detour, laddie."

"That might be so, Nanna, but we missed taking the last turning."

Rachael lifted a hand off the steering wheel and waved it about. "It's fine. I know what I'm doing. I found a shortcut that we'll be taking. I checked out the directions you gave me on the map, and I found there's a much quicker route through this estate. Being in the car for hours wastes the day."

"Oh, I've never been a different way to get to my home. Though normally I go by train and bus and my mum collects me from the station. The estate, is that Grosvenor? They're very particular about anyone going on to their land."

"Don't be silly laddie, they'll be fine. It wouldn't be on the map as an alternative route, would it now?"

I shrugged. "Oh, I suppose if it's on the map, then it's fine." The conversation in the front of the car continued as they argued about which road to take next.

After another thirty minutes in the car, I asked, "Are we lost?" It seemed like we were lost. We'd entered through some huge wrought iron gates that clearly had a no trespassing sign on them.

"No, this is the way. Your mum's home should be just over the other side of this estate," Rachael stated as a man appeared in front of us, waving his hands at us and clearly wanting us to stop. The guy was dressed in what looked like old fashioned gamekeeper clothing I'd seen in a movie.

"He looks like he's stepped off a movie screen," I said as the man glowered at us when Rachael brought the car to a stop.

Nanna glanced back, grinning. "My thoughts exactly. Let's hope he hasn't got a shotgun and tries to use us for target practice."

My eyes widened on the man. "He's not got a gun."

Nanna roared with laughter. "I hope not. Let's see if he can give us directions." The whir of the electric window going down was followed by a loud shout. "Excuse me, can you tell us which way it is to Elise's tepee. It's around here somewhere, and we're late."

Emotions too many to name crossed the guy's face while he walked to the window. His jaw bunched as he bent to look in through the window. "This is private land. You need to turn around and leave."

"There was nothing on the map to indicate we couldn't drive through here, so stop being pompous. Is chivalry dead around here?"

The man's mouth opened, but all that came out was a strangled noise.

"We don't have all day. Do you know which way we have to go to Elise's or not?" Nanna snapped out.

"As I've said, this is private land, and you're trespassing. You need to leave, now," he gritted out, a scowl rigidly fixed in place.

Nanna tutted loudly. "Now, what harm are we doing, laddie?" Before the man could respond, Nanna opened the car door, causing him to hop back to avoid being hit.

"Erm, Nanna, maybe we should just turn around," I offered helpfully.

She didn't appear to hear me as she got out of the car. "We know that the place we want to get to is here." Nanna pointed back to Rachael. "I have it on good authority we are in the right place. Now, are you going to be helpful, or do I need to ring Griffin Hudson, my future grandson-in-law?" Her hands went to her waist, her foot tapping on the ground.

Had Charlie and Griffin got engaged?

The guy's face went a rather deep shade of purple as he spluttered, "Griffin Hudson?"

"That's what I said. I see you've heard of him. He's a powerful man, you know. Grif is head over heels for my Charlie boy. It's a gay for you thingy, or so the thingmabob says.

They're a couple, you know, the kind that likes to get—"

"Dear Lord, please stop. Get in the car, and I'll walk you to the gate." He sounded equal parts terrified of Nanna continuing and frustrated at having given in.

When Nanna turned to give us a big thumbs up, Grumpy Guy said, "I haven't got all day."

My phone started to ring as Nanna got back in the car. "Rachael, follow him."

I looked at the screen with a sinking heart. "Hello, Mum."

"Where the heck are you, boy? Marcus arrived ages ago. What a wonderfully attractive man he is." I could hear Marcus's laughter in the background.

He's laughing; that had to be a good sign? Or was it hysteria?

"We're in the estate that borders your land. This man is walking us to you. We're not walking, he is. We're more driving at a snail kind of kangaroo pace," I corrected as Rachael inched forward, and the car started to jump like a kangaroo.

"I'll head to the gate and meet you there." The call ended a second later, with no chance for me to ask to speak to Marcus. Fifteen minutes later, after the guy walked us through the estate, past a huge mansion, and around the back down another long drive, I could see Mum and Marcus standing by an open gate.

"Does Marcus look happy?" I asked, the panic returning at seeing him alone with Mum.

Nanna twisted in her seat to glance at me. "He's grinning. What's the issue, laddie?"

I'd warned them all Mum was different; I just never expected Marcus to get any time alone with her. "Mum's different. She can be a little hard to cope with."

Nanna reached a hand back to me. I sat forward to take hold of it. "Listen to me. That man is head over heels for you. Your mum won't put him off regardless of her eccentricities. We all have them. Some are just more gifted with them than others."

I didn't disagree; I had plenty. "He told me he loves me."

The hand holding mine squeezed tighter. "Why are we only hearing about this now?"

"I'm still thinking about it. It's a lot to take in when you make your feelings known to someone. How do you know it's real? I mean, it feels real. The butterflies playing tag in my stomach say there's something different about my relationship with Marcus, but can we really rely on them? The life of a butterfly is so short. How can you measure your feelings against them?"

Nanna chortled. "You think too much, laddie. Love isn't something you can analyse, it just is. There is no rhyme nor reason to it. I'll ask you this. Does he make your heart sing when you're with him?"

"My heart has never been able to sing, Nanna. I'm not sure that's even possible, it's an organ, but not the kind that makes music. Although I suppose it does make music of sorts when it beats. It sets different rhythms. Oh, I'm wrong, Nanna, a heart can sing. Do you think mine will be in tune with Marcus's because, truth be told, I'm not a very good singer at all..." I met her sparkling eyes and stopped talking, heat crawling up my neck.

"You're a wonder laddie. I'm so glad Charlie introduced us. And yes, I'm very sure your heart matches Marcus's rhythm." The genuine sincerity of her words left me feeling a warm glow in the centre of my chest.

Rachael stopped the car and glanced sideways with a furrowed brow. "When you two have quite finished, Grumpy Guy is waving us on. One of you will need to get out to judge the gap. The gateway looks a little small to fit a car through."

"I'll do it." I got out and smiled politely at the man, but I'd not taken more than three steps when Marcus was through the gate and strode to me. "Sorry about all th—"

Marcus's mouth pressed against mine in a kiss that made the world disappear. The worry I'd been carrying around since he dropped me home three days ago, that our mutual declarations of love may somehow not have been real, disappeared. His mouth was hot and possessive. My hands crept around his waist so I could get closer to his warm, scented body.

"Finlo, put the man down."

Mum's voice was like a dash of ice-cold water, and I jerked, preparing to step back, only Marcus held on to me. His eyes were alight with wickedness that set my pulse racing, and that had no place in front of the ladies. "Please don't look at me like that."

His laughter was rich. "Like what?"

"I'm sure we've had this conversation before. Only then *I* was about to meet *your* mum."

"We might have." He kissed the end of my nose and kept his arm around my waist.

Nanna, who hadn't closed her window, shouted out, "Fin, put Marcus down for a minute, you're supposed to be helping."

"I need to check the width of the gate." I left Marcus's side to walk to the front of the car. Eyeing it and the open gate, I ran a hand through my hair. How to do this?

I looked at the gravel road and shrugged, then laying down, I called to Marcus. "Can you check my length next to the car?"

Marcus's face appeared over the bonnet of the car to look down at me, a breath-taking smile on his face. "One in a million, that's what you are."

"Isn't he just," Mum said.

CHAPTER TWENTY-ONE

Marcus

The thirty minutes I'd had with Elise had been illuminating, to say the least. The woman was a force of nature, and Fin had been right about picking a topic of conversation. Wisely, I'd listened and picked Fin as the topic. I'd heard all about how he'd been bullied at school, how he'd not fitted in the school system. That they'd tried to pigeonhole him and assess him with tests that, as far as Elise was concerned, would have limited him. Home-schooling for her had been the only option, and it seemed to have worked, though she'd been very vocal about Fin's desire to go to university. She clearly didn't approve. He'd had to have a test to assess his academic ability, which he'd passed with flying colours, yet she felt her son was limiting himself by going into higher education.

A lot of what she said made sense, and Fin had obviously benefitted from her tutelage, but she was also rigid in her thinking. What had made Fin need to go to uni to obtain his master's degree? From what Elise said, he was excelling.

Why had Fin never mentioned how he was getting on?

"Are you helping me?" called up the man in question from his spot on the ground. He'd moved from the front of Agnes's car and was now lying between the gate posts on the ground, trying to measure the length in relation to the car.

My lips quivered as I bent to try and judge the gap for Fin. "It looks like the car should get through."

Agnes, who'd decided to get out of the car, looked at the gate. "Let's leave it here. I think that's best."

There was a strangled noise from the man who'd remained, silently watching us as if we'd all lost the plot. "As I've explained, this is private land, it is not a car park. You'll need to drive through and go back to the main road."

Nanna glanced about, the smile on her face indicating she was up to something, but it was Elise who spoke up first. "Gavin, stop being a snobbish arse. The car isn't doing any harm by remaining here." She nodded up towards the house, which was partially hidden by trees. "They aren't home right now, are they? So it's not like they're going to notice."

Something passed over the man's face, and I got the distinct impression there was some sort of silent communication between him and Elise before he slowly nodded. "An hour, no more," he said, stalking off without looking at anyone.

"Is he always like that?" Fin asked.

Elise rolled her eyes, but her lips formed into a smile that I'd seen often on Fin's face. "On occasion. He takes his job as groundskeeper seriously. He also wants to preserve the environment, though, so he's not all bad." She waved at Rachael, who was still in the car. "Leave the car. It's only a ten-minute walk to the tepee."

It was difficult to keep a straight face when I glanced down at my now muddy boots, then at both Nanna and Rachael, who'd clearly dressed up for the occasion. This was going to be interesting.

Fin seemed to have a similar thought. "Mum, is it muddy? Nanna and Rachael don't have hiking boots on—"

"We'll be fine laddie, a bit of dirt never hurt anyone," Agnes said as she took hold of Elise's arm and started to fire questions at her.

"How long have you lived out here? Why did you choose the outskirts of London? How do you cope with an outside toilet in the winter? I imagine that's got to be hard."

"It gets very hard," Fin answered. "It's really difficult to clean out the toilet when everything is frozen solid." He sighed and took hold of my hand.

With difficulty, I kept my humour to myself, though Nanna and Rachael weren't shy and laughed loudly. Elise had shown me around what was essentially a large campsite, and I'd tried to envision what it would be like to live in the tepee all year round as Fin had done. "Did you enjoy living in the tepee?"

"Why wouldn't he enjoy it?" Elise answered before Fin could speak. "He got to be at one with nature and the elements. His carbon footprint was kept to a minimum, and he got to learn all about how to protect his surroundings. Every day was a learning opportunity."

Fin shrugged. "You learn a lot out here. Though it is nice to have water deeper than a bowl to wash my backside in."

Nanna laughed. "Laddie, you're a brave one."

He grinned. "Nanna, I've told you silver foxes only live in North America, so I wasn't really brave. There is nothing out here to hurt me."

I frowned and looked between Agnes and Fin. "Silver foxes?"

"Yes, Nanna was worried they'd bite her backside when she had to use the outside loo," Fin explained.

My lips twitched again, and this time it was harder to hold back the laughter, but once more, the others gave in and laughed. I couldn't resist kissing Fin when his nose wrinkled. "I love you."

"What's this nonsense?" Elise stated, stopping in the middle of a boggy area, seemingly unconcerned for everyone else's feet.

Was that concern I could see?

"I wouldn't call my feelings for your son nonsense."

"Why would it be anything but good news?" Nanna questioned. "Young Fin is a catch, not that you're not too Marcus," she said, giving me a wink. "I think they make a perfect pair."

My smile brightened. "I can't argue with that."

Elise didn't seem to agree as she looked at Fin. "Fin is special."

The way it was said could have been interpreted many ways and left me defending what I damn well knew I felt for the wonderful man who was standing next to me, his expression filled with worry. "I know, and it's a part of why I love him."

Elise didn't appear to be deterred. "What is love?"

Oh, Christ!

How the hell did I explain that?

Fin spoke up before I could find something to say. "Nanna and I talked about this in the car. It's the heart singing to match the other person's rhythm. Mine matches Marcus's. Isn't that right, Nanna?"

"Absolutely." Agnes patted Elise's arm. "Marcus is a good man and will treasure your son."

"That's to be seen. Love is an unproven phenomenon. How can you measure something that's not tangible? Lust, on the other hand, is easier to define. It's a mixture of chemical reactions that are triggered by the sexual chemistry between two living things. Love is something created by the masses to generate financial reward."

Fin cringed and attempted to drop my hand. I clung to his fingers and squeezed gently. "I don't believe that, Elise. What I feel for your son is so much more than lust. I won't deny I find your son physically attractive, but it's not the only thing. I'm also drawn to his intellect, to how he sees the world as a whole. Those things aren't about lust. They're about the feelings he evokes in me."

It was at that exact moment Nanna's foot sank into a boggy bit of ground, and her arms flailed, trying to keep her upright. In what felt

216

like slow motion, I dropped Fin's hand and lurched forward to grab her before she fell. Aware that she'd broken her hip a while back, I didn't think twice about trying to stop her from falling. Only, I underestimated her weight, so the two of us wobbled precariously on the slippery mud. Seeing no way out as we headed towards the ground, I twisted so Agnes would land on me rather than the mud.

We landed hard in a heap of arms and legs, my arse taking the full brunt of the hit. Agnes made a grunting sound as the pain registered, and I called out, "Fuck, I think I've broke my arse."

As I struggled to catch my breath, Agnes pressed me down harder into the mud as she tried to gain a better purchase on me.

Seconds later, Fin crouched in front of us, a look of concern on his face. "Is it possible to break your arse?"

I couldn't help it, laughter wheezed out as Agnes lay against me, her body shaking.

"If he has, you're going to have to take good care of him," Agnes choked out past her laughter.

"I'm not a nurse, but I'm sure there'll be some information on the internet to help me."

That did it. I reached out a dirty hand and touched Fin's cheek. "I'm keeping you." The disgruntled tutting coming from his mother was ignored.

After our muddy mishap, Elise had let the subject of *'love'* drop, but I got the feeling we'd be returning to the topic at some point. We all managed to get to Elise's so I could clean a little of the mud off. The afternoon had been cut short when I'd gone to sit and realised how painful my backside actually was. It didn't take long to figure out that I'd done some damage to myself. As I was leaving, Elise had garnished me with a bag of herbs she suggested I put in hot water and drink as they had healing properties. Exactly what they were was still to be determined.

One visit to the emergency department that Agnes insisted on proved just how right I'd been about my arse.

Fin pulled up outside my house and switched off the engine. "That was interesting."

I chuckled at his understatement. "You can say that again." I didn't even attempt to look at the car seat, which I was sure was covered in mud as I got out of the car. My backside complained with every step I took. It would appear it was, in fact, possible to break one's backside. I'd fractured my tailbone, and sitting was no longer a pleasurable experience.

Agnes had been full of apologies after Fin had called as per her instructions when we'd left the hospital. Her offer to come and stay with me had been declined. Fin had been clear. He would be the one to stay and look after me. He'd driven us home, and I'd learnt that he loved to drive but couldn't afford a car.

"Wait for me," Fin called as I hobbled up the path to the house.

I didn't stop but called back, "I'm all right walking. It's the sitting that's the problem." It wasn't just the sitting. However, Fin's ghostly complexion and deep lines around his eyes and mouth kept me quiet about the latter. The last thing I wanted to do was make him worry more.

He was breathless when he reached me, carrying all the things from the hospital, along with the stuff Elise had insisted I needed to help me heal naturally. Right now, all I wanted was pain medication, a hot bath, and some food, in that order. After opening the door, Fin followed me inside. "What do you need me to do for you first?"

"Kiss my arse better?" I said flippantly as I stopped to shrug off my jacket.

A second later, hands took hold of my hips, and I felt the press of what had to be Fin's lips against my bum of the dirty trousers. My heart flipped over in my chest; I was sure of it. The simple gesture was more precious than anything anyone had ever done for me before. I sucked in a shaky breath as I glanced over my shoulder and down at the man kneeling behind me. There was a smear of mud on his lips and a streak of dirt on his cheek. God, he was so damn adorable.

"Did it help?" The earnest expression made my eyes ache.

I nodded, unable to speak past the lump of emotion in my throat. His eyes brightened. "What do you want to do first? Bath, pills or food?"

"Pills, then bath," my lips tilted up. "You might be in need of one too. But I know of a great way to conserve water." I gave him a saucy wink. "We can share."

His eyes twinkled with mirth. "That's a very good idea."

I couldn't agree more.

CHAPTER TWENTY-TWO

Fin

Between Nanna and Pippa, they'd had me covered for my stay in London. Pippa had packed a bag of clothes and my books. Nanna had somehow got Griffin to drop them off at Marcus's. I'd not mentioned to any of them I'd had to quit my job as a server in Billie's smoothie shop. I had enough to get me through if I was careful.

Pippa was going to share her notes with me for the classes I was missing so I could keep up. I'd put in an application for a couple of weeks leave of absence from attending classes. I could have skipped them, but it didn't feel right. That had been the easy part to sort after Marcus had argued he'd be fine alone and I should head back to Brighton on the first night.

He wasn't fine, and as it turned out, he wasn't a great patient either. Like right now, he was glowering at me as I offered to help.

"I've told you I can do that," Marcus snapped grumpily.

Who knew an injured Marcus would be so impatient? "Yes, I heard you. This," I pulled what I thought was the expression Marcus wore when he tried to crouch down, "is what you do when you try to bend down."

He ran a hand over his messy hair, his eyes narrowing on me. "I don't look like that."

Nodding, I picked up the photo that he'd dropped on the floor and handed it to him. He snatched it and laid it back on the large pile that sat on the low table I'd moved closer to him. "Maybe I'm not doing a good enough impression. I'll work on it for you."

Steve, who'd been sitting at his office desk not more than four feet away, burst out laughing. "He's right. You do look like that."

"Fuck off."

"Great comeback, grumpy knickers." Steve grinned at me.

"I don't think knickers can be grumpy. They can get in a twist, though."

The laughter returned, and Steve sat back in his chair. "You're right. Marcus has definitely got his in a twist this last week."

My brow furrowed. "Yes, but he's in pain from his broken arse." That got more laughter and not from Marcus.

"You pair do realise I'm right here?" Marcus said, his scowl deepening.

Steve shook his head. "It's not like we can miss you, is it? You've been a misery all week. I think Fin deserves a medal for putting up with you twenty-four seven."

"Can you get a medal for that?" Marcus heaved a very loud sigh, and I stroked a hand up his leg. "Do you want some more tablets? Or maybe some of the herbal tea?"

"Jesus, no, that stuff tastes like sewer water." Marcus shuddered.

"How do you know what sewer water tastes like? Surely that's a severe health risk to drink. I'm sure I've read that consuming human waste can make you very sick." It was my turn to shudder.

"I was being rhetorical."

"Oh. So do you want some herbal tea? It's good for you."

Steve made several choking noises, but when I glanced in his direction, he was looking down, and I couldn't make out what his problem was.

Marcus took hold of my hand. "No, but thank you. The tea is awful, and right now, I just want to try and get on with going through some of these photos. I need to decide what the narrative should be, to go with each of them for my next book. My publisher is hassling, and as usual, I've left this in the to-do pile for so long that it's become urgent."

The pile of pictures he indicated stood at least five inches high. There was a notepad next to the stack, and the page was blank. "Can I help?"

One brow rose. "You want to help me pick the photos for the book?"

"I'm not sure I'm qualified to pick those, though it was nice of you to offer. No, I was thinking more about the narration to go with what you pick." I held up the photo on top of the pile, which Marcus had just dropped on the floor. I inspected it carefully, placing it in front of me on top of my own pad I'd been using to write in before Marcus had tried to bend down. The image was in black and white, showing what appeared to be some sort of important historical site that had been bombed out. "What can you tell me about where you were? What was it about this place that drew your attention?"

Marcus sat back, winced, and shifted on the egg cushion he'd bought to help when he was sitting. "This was in Mali in two-thousand-nineteen." His onyx eyes appeared to lose focus as he stared at the image. "There'd been a peace deal signed in two-thousand-thirteen, but it hadn't changed much for those people or the country as a whole. I was given a brief to go in and document some of the atrocities.

It wasn't just about the death. It was about the destruction of those things that were held as significantly important to the people."

"It was a shit show, that's what it was," Steve muttered.

"Islamic extremists attacked and damaged or destroyed historical sites on the grounds that they said were idolatrous, particularly in Timbuktu. A UNESCO World Heritage site was burned. They destroyed the tomb of a Sufi saint." He tapped at the picture. "This was supposed to be protected." The sigh he gave was heartfelt. "They also attacked several other sites in Timbuktu with pickaxes and shovels. Over a hundred soldiers died that year trying to stop this nonsense. Fuck knows what the total casualty count was as the war continues still." He moved forward, his hands running over his face and up into his hair.

If I wasn't mistaken, tension rolled off him, and Steve didn't appear much better as he sat upright in his seat, staring at Marcus with an unhappy expression. "Countries through the centuries remain full of the scattered remains and harsh realities of war. What is attacked are those things that hold belief and hope. Saints, according to the Catholic Church, are anyone in heaven who may have not always lived perfect lives, but amid their faults and failings, kept moving forward to prove they wanted to please their Lord.

"That is all about a belief that is inherent in culture and has nothing to do with actual visual artefacts. Belief and hope can't be destroyed through destruction of property, but it can be empowered to unite those in a shared goal." I tapped at the picture. "This isn't always about destruction, but about the hope born from it."

Marcus had turned his head to stare at me with an expression I couldn't read. "There are times, like now, when you transport me to see past the carnage." His eyes held an intensity as a hand came up and stroked my cheek. "I love you."

A wave of heat ran up my neck as Steve silently got up and clapped me on the shoulder before he left the room. I tilted my head, the hand falling away. "Why's he leaving?"

"He's giving us some space. Come here."

I looked at the inch separating us. "I'm already pretty close."

He chuckled. "Not nearly close enough." To that, he shifted, his face didn't mask the wince, but he didn't stop. I was bodily pulled off my seat and dragged onto Marcus's lap.

"I don't think this is a good—" I didn't get any further as Marcus's lips pressed against mine in a soft kiss that made me sigh. His tongue touched my lips, encouraging me to open, to allow him to deepen the kiss. The second I did, his tongue traced over mine. The flavour of the coffee he'd drunk was there, but also his familiar taste. I groaned as he sucked my tongue into his mouth, his hands sliding under my T-shirt to caress my spine.

The groans and moans increased to the point I wasn't sure who they were coming from. Marcus's arousal pressed against my arse and tempted me to grind down. The full week I'd been here, sharing a bed with him, we'd done no more than kiss and cuddle because Marcus couldn't seem to find a comfortable spot in the bed to do anything more. It had been a whole new experience to share a bed, and there be no sex. I liked it a lot. And it seemed Marcus had as well, the way he'd wrapped his body around mine most nights, snuggling his face into the back of my neck.

"Want you so bad," Marcus rasped as his mouth travelled down the side of my neck. His whiskers rubbing against my skin, flooding it with sensations that got my body responding.

"I...aren't...working..." I gave up as his lips started to suction at the junction between the base of the neck as one hand came around the front of my top to play with one of my nipples.

His mouth returned to mine, and any thoughts of stopping disappeared as his mouth hungrily ate at mine. The kiss was full of passion.

"Christ, I gave you some alone time to *talk*, not to have a make-out session." Steve's voice cut through the haze of desire like a knife.

Wriggling on Marcus's lap to escape wasn't my best idea as his erection rubbed against my backside, drawing a low growl from him.

"Jeez, honest, I'm not into a sex show. Should I just pack up and leave you to it?"

"Go home, Steve," Marcus murmured, not even bothering to look at the other man. Hungry eyes kept my gaze as the fingertips teasing my nipple continued to keep me distracted.

There was noise and what sounded like several huffy sighs before a door slammed, but Marcus didn't stop what he was doing with his mouth and hands. It was a losing battle to keep a conscious thought in my head. Marcus's backside might not like something too energetic, regardless of what his cock wanted.

When he released my mouth, I took hold of his face and took a couple of deep breaths as my heart continued to pound excitedly. "We have to be sensible."

Lines appeared around his eyes as he laughed. "I don't want to be sensible. I want to strip you off and fuck you over Steve's desk."

"I don't think he'd like that very much."

Marcus's eyes sparked wickedly. "He doesn't need to know."

I blinked owlishly. Was he serious? "What about I ride your cock right here while you sit on your egg cushion?"

"I'm sure that even saying egg cushion, in the same sentence as riding your cock, isn't sexy in the least." Marcus's body shook with the laughter that followed.

I sighed. "Yeah, it's not really sexy. But what else could I have said? Egg sitter doesn't sound any better, does it? Or even orthopaedic support for tailbone pain."

Marcus was shaking so hard he nearly dislodged me as he continued to laugh. "This, right here, is why I love you so goddamn hard."

My nose wrinkled. "Because I ramble stupid facts?"

He shook his head. "They aren't stupid. What you do is try to find the rational option that suits best. There is nothing wrong with that, and it makes me crazy about you."

"Okay."

His arms wrapped around me, and he pulled me against his chest, nestling my head under his chin. The sexual tension abated for the moment and was replaced with something much more potent, intimacy.

"I love when you hold me like this."

His lips brushed over the top of my head. "Me too."

CHAPTER TWENTY-THREE

Marcus

Ever since I'd asked Steve to leave Fin and me alone the week before, a thought had taken root, and over the last several days, it had morphed into something more tangible. Fin had a wonderful perspective on how he viewed my images. His love of history came through in the long discussions we'd had, and he'd given me new insight into my work, which left me contemplating offering him a job. It was obvious to me he'd make a great researcher and narrator for my work. He'd be able to use his unique view of life, and his passion for history, to help with the gallery shows and the planned books I'd committed to publishing.

I'd not mentioned it as yet, wanting to talk to Steve about it to see what his thoughts were on it. Over the years, I'd come to value and trust his opinion. Today, Fin had given me the opportunity to speak freely with Steve as he'd gone upstairs into the main house to do some of his own coursework. It appeared I was too much of a distraction.

I chuckled.

"What are you laughing at?"

I glanced up at Steve, who was in the process of clearing his desk. It was early Friday afternoon, and as I'd had to cancel some of the planned work over the last couple of weeks, Steve had requested to take some extra time off to spend with his boyfriend. I just needed a few minutes before he left.

"I was thinking about Fin," I answered honestly.

He stopped what he was doing and pointed at me. "That's not new."

I grinned. "Nope, but offering him a job is."

Steve came around his desk and perched on the seat next to me, his face wearing a serious expression. "This is news. You thinking of getting rid of me?"

My smile disappeared at the hint of apprehension he'd not masked. "Steve, you've been my right-hand man for years. I think we've established that you're indispensable to me."

A slow smile spread over his face, right along with a rosy blush. "That's some compliment. Does it come with a pay rise?" He winked cheekily at me, going for a hopeful look.

"Cheeky fucker, I already pay you over the odds."

He shook his head, a smug look appearing on his face. "I'm worth every penny. You just said so."

"I take it back."

He held up his hand. "Too late. Anyway, if you're not going to give me a pay rise, let's go back to the subject of you offering Fin a job. What do you have in mind?"

I sat back and was relieved to note that I barely felt any pain in my arse. Templing my fingers under my chin, I stared at the pile of pictures I'd set aside, which now included several pages of notes that Fin had made. "Last week when you left early—"

"When you told me to leave, if memory serves me right, all 'cause you wanted to do the nasty," Steve pointed out before I could finish.

I glanced at his desk, letting my gaze linger. He looked at me, then his desk and back. "You never!"

Shrugging, I barely held on to the laughter at the look of horror forming on his face. "I might have if Fin had agreed."

That afternoon had ended with Fin on his knees between my legs. Not quite what I'd wanted for either of us, but I'd repaid him the following morning by giving him a rimming he'd likely not forget for a while, judging by the way he'd covered the bed sheets in cum.

Steve shuddered, his eyes narrowing on me. "You're thinking about sex, aren't you."

"Maybe."

"Get your head out of your underwear. I pity Fin, I do. At least one of you has a moral compass."

I snorted. "Listen to who's talking. Did you or did you not have sex in your parents' bed?"

He rolled his eyes at me. "I'm never getting drunk with you again."

"Is it my fault you get loose lips after a few gins? Anyway, let's go back to Fin. Otherwise, you'll still be here in an hour. Fin has been going through the photos I've chosen for my next book, and he's been doing some background research on where the pictures were taken, then adding what I now call a "Finism" to each one."

The laughter was expected. "Finism, is that a euphemism for something else?"

"Piss off, and no, it's not. He's real insight, and I adore how he views the world." I got serious. "That last shoot we did in Alegria, it took something from me, something I didn't think I'd get back."

He nodded slowly. "The passion."

It was my time to nod. "That and a chunk of my heart." I rubbed at the centre of my chest, recalling the first conversation Fin and I'd had about the images hurting me. "It hurts, and Fin was the first to say it aloud to me. It made me see that the pain, in some way, was my penance for being a part of something bigger than me that I can't fix. But in a way, documenting what's happening is me honouring those who've suffered."

He sniffed and wiped the back of his hand over his nose. "You're going to continue, aren't you?"

"After Alegria, it was a hard no, but now I'm not so sure. It's a possibility." I looked at him closely. "How do you feel about that?"

Deep lines appeared around his mouth, his expression grim. "I'm not sure. I felt the same after that last little escapade. I'll need to give it some thought."

"I understand. It isn't an all or nothing offer, Steve. Staying here and running things is enough to keep you busy, so I'm not going to pressure you into doing something you don't want."

His smile returned. "Thanks, I appreciate that. I'll give it some thought and let you know." He got up and stared at me for a moment. "Fin, he's good for you. For a time, I was worried you'd never find someone, given how easily you always got bored with the guys you dated. He seems to give you something

235

that was missing from the other relationships. I'm happy for you both." He clapped me on the shoulder, saying nothing more as he went to finish what he was doing.

I sat silently, mulling over his words. Fin was good for me; it was true. He was much like an onion full of layers, only each one held a different surprise. Unwrapping those layers created a constant change that was never boring. He had the ability to shift how I perceived things, and that, in a way, was a gift I was coming to treasure on a daily basis.

Two weeks, he'd been under my roof, and I'd discovered how easily he slotted into my life as if he'd always been there. The depth of my feelings at odd moments astonished me. I'd known I was capable of love, just not the deep, enduring kind. The kind that I was coming to understand I felt for Fin and couldn't imagine living without now I'd experienced it.

Did I want to go back to the way it was before, seeing each other maybe once or twice a week? Did I shite. I wanted...him here, with me. That created the issue of how I broach that subject with Fin, who was bound to be thinking about heading back to Brighton. It had already been nearly two full weeks. Could he be convinced to stay longer?

You mean forever, don't you?

I barely contained a sigh as I swallowed and eyed Steve as he threw the leather strap of his bag over his shoulder. "Have a good weekend."

His smile was full. "I'll do my best. Speak to Fin, and we'll talk again on Monday. Good luck," he said as I watched him go, leaving me with my thoughts.

Yesterday, I'd woken to find Fin nestled into my side, and I'd lain staring at his sleeping form for a long time. The realisation I wanted to start every day with him in my arms wasn't surprising. What was, however, was the lengths I'd considered going to. Marriage wasn't something I'd ever really given much thought to, yet I could now see it in my future. Achieving that right now seemed a little unrealistic and made my stomach knot, thinking about those future conversations. Just how far in the future was the question.

Right now, the part of me that didn't like to wait for anything was battling with the cautious part that didn't want Fin to run a mile. We'd not gone back over the conversation about his mother's perception of love. And if I was honest, I was secretly worried about what it meant to Fin. He'd expressed himself and declared his feelings, yet the memory of him trying to pull away when the subject had been brought up by Elise niggled in the back of my mind.

Was it too soon to ask him to move in? Was it selfish to ask him to commute daily to Brighton? That I could easily afford to buy him a car didn't matter. Fin's acceptance of such a gift would be the issue. Money wasn't a problem as long as I didn't go overboard. Just last week, he'd left money on the kitchen counter to help pay towards the food I'd had delivered, which said a lot about the person he was. A car was out of the question. The idea of me moving to Brighton, that wasn't going to work either. My diary was absolutely packed, having had to do a lot of rescheduling recently. Fuck, that meant I'd have even less time with Fin if he went back to Brighton.

I slumped in my seat and chewed my lower lip between my teeth. It was only a month until finals; I could survive that, couldn't I? I shut my eyes at the sinking feeling in the pit of my stomach. I was pathetic.

There was a squeaking sound that alerted me to Fin's return. I glanced up, a smile already forming on my lips as he appeared. The smile was returned, and fuck if it didn't make my heart skip merrily in my chest and make the thought of him leaving all the harder. Dark hair was stuck up in several directions, and his baggy T-shirt hung off one milky white shoulder, having been stretched too many times to go back. He looked like a rag-a-muffin. I couldn't have loved him more right then. "I was getting lonely down here on my lonesome."

Fin glanced about the room. "Did Steve leave already? Have I lost track of time again?"

"No, you haven't. Steve went early." I patted the seat next to me, pretending not to notice how my hand trembled, my heart rate triple timing at what I was about to discuss. "Which I'm glad about 'cause I've something I want to talk about."

CHAPTER TWENTY- FOUR

Fin

I stared out of the train window, paying no attention to the passing scenery, my mind on the conversation I'd had with Marcus the day before and my awful decision to visit my mum to discuss my future. As the one person I'd always gone to talk through any major decisions with, at the time, it had seemed like the logical decision to visit her this morning.

The trip to see her had been...*a disaster*. Her words continued to replay through my head on repeat.

"Love is a myth Fin, get your head out of the clouds. Have I taught you nothing? Marcus will grow tired of you, and then where will you

be? As for working together, it sounds like a made-up job so he can keep you right where he wants you. He's already got you running around after him. He's controlling you. I thought I'd taught you better than to get yourself mixed up with someone like that."

"Mum, it's not like that. I offered to look after him. How is that controlling?" A sliver of doubt wormed its way in. Had I got it wrong?

No...no, I hadn't. Marcus isn't like that.

Her eyes narrowed. "He should be healed by now with what I gave him. Therefore he's keeping you there to run around after him for no reason other than to use you."

I shook my head. "Not everyone wants to use herbal remedies. He doesn't like the taste. And he hates that I have to run around after him. Half the time, we have to have a discussion as to why I'm helping." The frustration was there, and it was making it hard to make sense of what was happening.

"See, you don't match, regardless of what he says. This proves it."

I stared at her, unable to see her logic. "How does this prove anything? Mum, I'm confused. We've talked about this before. It's all right to think differently. Isn't that what you taught me when I was growing up? Why did you insist I'd be better off here so you could teach me properly if you aren't going to stand by that? What has changed? Why can't

He's rich, mega-rich. Did that have any bearing on our relationship?

Mum seemed to think so. Was money the root of all evil? And did that necessarily mean that Marcus was evil? I couldn't see it. There was something about the man's photography that portrayed the heart of him. It was there in the images that were so full of emotions. Emotions he didn't hide from.

Yet Mum seemed to think the worst of him. She was wrong. I was convinced of it. Marcus was good, and though I couldn't explain love any better than a hallmark card, something inside me recognised that what we had was special. *Then why are you questioning everything now?*

Was it the years I'd spent listening to my mum? She'd been wrong about uni, so was she wrong on this score too? I'd never been able to convince her that going to uni was something good for me. Was I going to be able to convince her that Marcus was good for me too? Did it even matter?

The ache in the centre of my chest suggested it did. Could I live with it if we disagreed over this? I'd lived with the disapproval over school. Would this be different?

My feet seemed to have taken the decision on where I should head, with my mind occupied by the worries. Standing in front of

Charlie's home, I sighed and walked the last few steps up to the front door.

After knocking, I stood back, half expecting there to be no one home on a Saturday afternoon, but Griffin opened the door, the scowl I'd got used to firmly in place. "Fin, hello. Are you after Charlie? He's gone out with Guy."

"Hi, no, I'm after Agnes."

"Sorry, she's out with Rachael."

"Oh, okay, thanks." Deflated, I turned to head back the way I'd come.

"Is there something I can help with?"

I stopped mid-turn to glance at Griffin. The man's face never gave much away, but something about his eyes said he was...*pissed off*? "Are you sure you want to help? You don't sound or look like you want to help?"

The lines on his forehead smoothed while his lips curled up at the edges. "You're not wrong. But do you want to come in and talk about whatever has you looking so glum?"

Was I looking glum? "I was looking to talk to Nanna about Mum's reaction to Marcus."

"And her reaction was what?"

"Not great. She thinks he's using me."

Rich laughter that changed the whole of Griffin's expression poured out of him. "Marcus, a user? Not in this lifetime. That man is one of the most generous men I know."

"Really?"

246

"Come in. I'm not standing on the doorstep having this conversation."

"Wasn't that exactly what we were doing?" I questioned as I followed Griffin inside.

His response was a grunt.

In the large, sunny room, he went and sat on the sofa, indicating I should take a seat. "What's the real issue here?"

The bluntness helped. "Mum doesn't believe in love. That's number one. Second, she thinks that Marcus's job offer is bogus so that he can have me running around after him, like a slave. Or something like that. Thirdly, he must be evil to have loads of money."

There was no laughter this time, but his lips did twitch. "Your mother sounds like she has some very... rigid and fixed ideas about certain things. But life isn't rigid or fixed, is it?"

The simplicity of his response undid the large knots in my stomach. "No, no, it isn't."

He sat back. "I've known Marcus for about ten years. In that time, I've never known him to flaunt his money, to use it for evil purposes, if that counts for anything. The charity he set up to help war refugees is one of the largest of its kind, and he's donated huge amounts of his money and time. Those are not the actions of a selfish man."

My nose wrinkled. "War refugee charities?"

One hand tapped on the arm of the sofa as Griffin met my stare. "He didn't tell you about it?"

I shook my head. "This is the first time I've heard about it."

"Then I'll say no more. You need to ask him about it." His hand stopped moving as he came forward. "Marcus is a good man. He's not prone to lying that I can tell, and other than a slightly warped sense of humour, he's a solid guy. One I count as a friend, and I don't have many of those."

"Me either. No one sticks around for long. I'm told I'm hard work."

Griffin scowled. "People are fools. You shouldn't listen to them."

I grinned. "Marcus said the same thing. You too are very alike."

His face flushed a dark pink as the scowl deepened. "Whatever. Have you spoken to Marcus about these concerns?"

"I left Mum's to come home, to give myself some thinking time. Only I found myself here. I was supposed to go back to Marcus's, but…"

"You got stuck in your head," he offered.

"Yeah, I suppose I did."

"My advice, for what it's worth? Go talk to Marcus."

Minutes later, I was heading back to the train station with yet more questions, but with a clearer head…*I think.*

CHAPTER TWENTY-FIVE

Marcus

Pacing in front of the window, I checked my wristwatch for the hundredth time. Where was Fin? He'd been gone over five hours. I'd done the maths, and by my calculation, he should have possibly been back here an hour ago.

The phone in my back pocket started to ring and stopped me pacing long enough to take it out and check the caller ID. "Hey, Griffin."

"I'm going to need to apologise," Griffin said, in his usual gruff tone without any preamble.

What?

"Why do you need to apologise?" I asked in confusion.

"Fin came by the house, and we had a chat—"

"Hang on, Fin is in Brighton?" My heart lodged itself in my throat at what would cause him to go home without saying anything.

"He was. I think he's on his way back to you."

"I'm lost. Why did he come to see you? And why do you think he's coming back?" My stomach churned. What was going on?

"He didn't. He came to speak with Agnes, but she was out. He looked...anyway, I somehow ended up having a conversation with him, and I mentioned the war charities you set up."

I exhaled noisily. "Why were you talking about that?"

"See, this is why I don't do people. It's Nanna. I'm sure the woman is rubbing off on me. Listen, he wanted to talk over some of the things about you and the misconceptions his mother has. I was trying to help."

The sheer exasperation set me off laughing. It was typical Griffin. "You were singing my praises."

"I was doing no such thing. I merely gave my opinion on whether or not I believed you to be evil."

Evil! "Oh Christ, his mother told him I was evil?"

"I don't think she meant you per se, more your association with money. It sounds like she has some pretty odd ideas about certain things."

"Yeah, I got that impression, but I thought I'd won her over when I went to meet her. I arrived early so I could lay some groundwork about how I felt about her son. She doesn't believe in love." I sighed as my palms started to sweat at what was going on inside Fin's head right now.

"It would appear so. Fin, for all his…" Griffin made a growly noise.

"He's hard to define, I get it. It's okay. Just give me the gist of the conversation, so I know what I'm dealing with."

Once I'd ended the call, I stared out the window, seeing nothing but Fin's face when he'd left this morning. The conversation the day before had not gone as I hoped.

"Are you offering me a job?" Fin's brows rose.

"Yes. I'm looking for an assistant—"

"Steve's your assistant."

I nodded. "True, I'm not after someone to do the same as Steve. He can easily manage the day to day stuff I require."

"Then why do you need an assistant then? Is this because I don't have any job prospects? As I told Mum, something will come up, I think."

A grin spread over my face. "If you give me a second, I'll explain." I waited, knowing he'd need to answer me.

"Okay."

"What it seems I'm not making clear is, I'm interested in employing you to work with me to research the history of where I've taken the pictures, to add another dimension to my work. The narrative, I want you to do, so that this book is different from the last few I've published."

His eyes brightened. "Wow, seriously? That's a way cooler job than I'd ever expect to get."

"Yep, seriously. And I think it's cool for someone who loves history to do the research. You see things with fresh eyes that are very energising. I've other books I've been commissioned to do, so this isn't just a one-off project. There are several exhibitions planned, and I'd want a similar depiction for each of the chosen images too. It's a lot of work and responsibility. There are deadlines. Right now, I've the next three years mapped out. So if you're worried this is a short term thing, it's not."

He got off the seat and started to pace in front of me. "You trust me with this?" he squeaked.

He didn't look at me, causing my stomach to lurch. "I do. Can you stop and look at me?"

It took a few seconds, but when he did, there were deep grooves at the sides of his mouth and one between his brows. "There are probably experts out there for this kind of thing. What if I fuck it up? What if—"

"What if's are for wusses," I said, trying to break the tension that seemed to be growing in the room.

"Wusses? What if that's what I am? What if I can't follow through. Mess stuff up? It happens, for me a lot."

I got off the seat, unable to watch his stress. "You've spent the last four years in uni and proven you can do anything you set your mind to. I have faith in you, Fin. I love you."

As I went to wrap my arms around him, he stepped back, and an ache developed just under my heart. "Will you still love me if I mess up, if I ruin something important?"

No matter what I'd said after that to reassure him that I would, he seemed to get into a panic I couldn't break him from. I'd spent around an hour trying to understand all his worries. It was the first time I'd seen the real influence his upbringing had on him.

As Griffin had pointed out, Fin's mother was rigid in her thinking. Up to now, Fin had been the exact opposite. Was this reaction because it was directly connected to his feelings?

Possibly. And if that was the case, then how could I make him see differently?

I rubbed at my bristly jaw with one hand, pulling my phone back out with the other. Not overthinking things, I dialled my mother.

"To what do I owe this pleasure?"

"Why does it have to owe to anything?" I chuckled at how it sounded much like a Fin question. He was rubbing off on me.

"Marcus, you rang me on Thursday to update me on your health. Normally, to garner two calls in a week, you usually want something."

My chuckles increased. "You've cottoned on to my dastardly plan."

"Marcus." That one word was filled with all the exasperation I'd come to expect.

"I love you." There was a small sound that sounded distinctly like a sob. "I don't tell you nearly enough. Or that I'm grateful for you being the mum you are."

This time, the sob was louder, then there was a moment of silence. "What's brought this on? Is everything all right?" Her voice was thick with emotion.

"I offered Fin a job, and he's...well, I'm not sure what he is, but he went home to see his mum, and she told him I was evil."

"She did *what?*" The outrage made the ear pressed to the phone ring.

I switched the phone to my other ear. "I would like my eardrums to remain intact."

"How dare she call you evil. What gives her the right. She's met you for what, an hour and a half?" She continued like I'd not said a word.

I tried again. "Mum."

"The audacity of the woman. I'll be having words with her about this. Give me her address."

The continued outrage took away a little of the hurt I was feeling at Fin not returning. "Okay, She-Ra, you can calm down now. Elise has a few fixed ideas about the wealthy. I'm not sure if there's a valid reason, or she's just made some huge assumptions about people with money. She lives on a bit of land she claimed through squatters rights."

"What have you got yourself mixed up in?"

"Mum, don't start that nonsense. Fin's upbringing and his mother have nothing to do with my feelings for him. You raised me better than that."

"Point taken," she conceded immediately. "Where is Fin now?"

I sighed dejectedly, deflating immediately. "He went to visit Elise and hasn't returned...what if she makes him believe there is no such thing as love?"

"Were we not talking about a job a second ago? What has this to do with love?"

"Again, she told Fin there is no such thing as love."

"Poppycock. Does she not love her son?"

I rubbed at my temple. "I didn't think about it from that angle. She has different views on things, but if you pushed me, I'd say she loves him. Though she'd probably come up with some other rationale about that."

There were a few seconds of silence. "Are you worried Fin doesn't know his own feelings? Is this what this is all about?"

"Maybe? But it's more than that. I was going to ask him to move in with me. I want him here with me. These past few weeks, even though I've been a shit to live with, he's not complained. Fuck, he's like a ray of sunshine. He can cast warmth onto anything. I love having him with me, I really don't want him to leave."

"Then what stopped you from asking him to move in?" That she didn't ask if it was too soon, released a little of the tension in my shoulders.

"He got a little consumed with trying to figure out all the reasons it wasn't good for him to work with me."

There was a discreet laugh. "I'm sure he did. The boy has an extraordinary mind."

It was my turn to laugh. "He does, and it's wonderful."

"I'll be honest, I had my doubts about the two of you, but he suits you somehow. Why don't you invite him and his mother over for Sunday lunch tomorrow and let me see if I can change her mind about a few things?"

My grin was back. "I knew I could count on you, Mum."

CHAPTER TWENTY-SIX

Fin

By the time I'd got back to Marcus's, I'd expected him to question where I'd been, only he hadn't. Instead, he'd asked me to call Mum and ask her if she'd join us for Sunday lunch. It had been the last thing I'd expected to happen, and I'd no clue why I'd done as he asked. She'd agreed and, fortunately, hadn't tried to continue our earlier conversation. I was still trying to make sense of it all. Both Mum and Marcus were... I was clueless.

Marcus had disappeared down to his dark room, not giving me a chance to talk about what was playing on my mind. Not that anything was playing as such, more like bullying my other thoughts and trying to get me to do something I'd not normally do. Like go down and disturb Marcus when he was in his dark room, something Steve had expressly said not to do if I didn't want to find out exactly what a real bear looked like on a tear. I'd not questioned why he thought Marcus resembled a bear. I mean, he did have hair on his body, but nothing like a real bear.

"Oh, stop it," I muttered and stomped to the stairs that lead down into the studio. The place was empty, and there was a red light filtering under the door of the room that Marcus used to develop his pictures. When he'd given me a tour of the house, it was the one room we'd not ventured into. He'd pointed it out but hadn't asked me to have a look inside.

Was there something secret in there? He'd been so open about showing me the rest of the place. Why not this room too? I scratched at my neck and tilted my head to listen. Met with silence, I walked to the door, my hand hesitating before I knocked.

"Yeah?" Marcus called out, his voice muffled by the door.

I raised my voice as I asked, "Can I come in?" I rolled my eyes to the ceiling. Why was I asking that? Maybe I should have asked him to come out? He clearly didn't want me to go in there. I shrugged at the strange need I felt to see what was behind the door. What secrets did it hold?

"Hang on."

I pressed my ear to the door and was sure I could hear several cuss words. What was wrong?

Three minutes later, the door opened, and the red light was now a normal bright white light. Marcus's expression was...that I wasn't totally sure about. Possibly sheepish? Maybe guilty? Why guilty? What would he have to be guilty about?

Then my gaze travelled around the room. It was bigger than I thought it would be. I'd somehow imagined it to be a poky space, but this was anything but. It had to be over twelve feet square, with a counter that took up the whole of the back wall, covered in trays and a massive sink. However, that wasn't what held my attention. It was the long length of strings hanging from the ceiling with...*holy fuck*. Before I understood what I was going to do, I stepped fully into the room. Unsure if I was blinking or not, I rubbed at my eyes just to check they were open and I wasn't having some weird dream.

My gaze remained on what must have been over fifty images of me. Some were from the fashion show that I'd not been aware Marcus had taken because I was in just my underwear. What caught my attention was the other pictures that he'd taken with my permission. I'd no clue why I'd not given any thought afterwards to the images. I could see now he'd taken way more pictures than I'd realised at the time.

The air seemed to have disappeared from the room as I got closer. Did I really look like that? The desire I'd felt was clearly evident on my face as well as through the underwear. I looked… "I don't look like that?" I blurted out when the word *sexy* popped into my head.

Marcus chuckled, his arm brushing against mine. The scent of chemicals became more obvious as he reached up and plucked a picture down off the string, holding it out to me. What his expression revealed caused my heart to swell and fill my chest. "Yes, you do. The camera doesn't lie. It has captured the real you. This is how I see you, my beautiful Fin." When I took the picture, he traced a fingertip over my cheekbone and down to the corner of my mouth as if he was memorising me. There was an intensity about him I was getting used to seeing. "I got a little carried away. It seems you've turned into my muse."

"I…I don't know what to say. How can that be? I always have something to say."

The rich laughter that I'd come to associate with Marcus, which always left me with a warm feeling, filled the room. "There is always a first time for everything." His lips brushed against mine, and the picture I held was forgotten.

The ability he had to make me forget myself was both a gift and a curse when I was sure I'd come down to see him with a purpose in mind. He deepened the kiss, and I dropped what I was holding to wrap my arms around him. I was dazed and slightly confused when I blinked and what appeared to be the bedroom into focus, sometime later, finding we were both half-naked and Marcus was kissing his way down my body.

"How..." I groaned and gave up trying to make sense of everything other than his mouth on me. His hands went to my belt buckle as he nibbled along the top of my jeans.

"Lift up," he murmured, his hot breath brushing over my sensitive skin. A shiver ran down my body as I did what he wanted. My jeans and underwear were gently pushed down my legs, and his mouth followed. His tongue licked at the junction of my thigh and groin, but he didn't touch my cock, which bucked in the warm air.

My clothes disappeared as he continued to worship me with his mouth and his hands. Words he'd previously said about worshipping me floated through my mind as he did just that. A sheen of sweat coated what had become super sensitive skin by the time he returned to kiss me deeply.

I ran my hands over his back as his body pressed fully against mine. Chest to chest, his warm skin and soft hair rubbed at mine, eliciting a moan he swallowed. His trousers stopped me from being able to rub my aroused cock against him like I wanted. His heart beat a fast tattoo that matched mine. There were more moans as I cupped his arse to hold him to me. Rolling my hips, it provoked a deep guttural groan that vibrated through me.

Minutes bled together, and the kisses turned more demanding, as did my need for more. I tugged at the waistband of his trousers impatiently. "Off, damn it. Please. I need you," I gasped between breaths, my chest heaving as he eased back. His deep flush of desire played havoc with the need to drag him back to me.

"So needy, my beautiful Fin." The growl was deep and sexy.

"Jeez, honestly, you need to be naked." A wicked smile followed and didn't help the situation at all. I wasn't very strong, but my impatience helped as I flipped him, tumbling Marcus onto his back. His laughter was breathless as his eyes gleamed like a polished stone. His hair was dishevelled from my hands, his lips swollen and slick from our kisses. "I love you. I don't understand it, but do I need to? I've no clue, but when I'm with you, everything just seems better."

His chest heaved while his hands came up to cup my face and bring me towards him. His breath ghosted over my face as he held me mere inches from him. Something that looked like uncertainty flashed over his face, then was gone. "Move in with me."

The hands holding me kept me from pulling back as I shook. "You…really?"

A smile that was full of…hope spread over his face. "Really. I wanted to ask you yesterday, but then we got stuck in the whole job thing." I opened my lips, and Marcus shook his head. "Let me say my piece first." He waited for me to answer as he always did.

As he always did! He gets me. He really gets me.

"You get me."

"I do, or I hope I do. I want to get you in every way, Fin. It might seem too quick, but fuck, you're it for me. I can't see myself with anyone but you. I'm selfish and greedy with you. I want you here with me. And before your brilliant mind starts to overthink and start connecting dots, I'm going to lay it all out for you. I offered you the job for two reasons. Firstly, so I could be with you more, and secondly, because you have talent that suits my work perfectly. If you choose to not move in with me…*just yet*, the job offer remains. Though I'm not promising not to push for both, I'm just saying."

It was said with such passion, I couldn't fail to believe him. The conversation with Mum sat there between us. "Mum disagrees with me working for you, with us loving each other."

"How do you feel about that?" he asked in an incredibly quiet voice.

The passion that had sizzled between us mere minutes ago disappeared at the seriousness of the conversation. "I'm upset that she can't see that this"—I pointed between us— "makes me happy. The job, I want it. I've loved doing the research and trying to figure out how you might view the image you took, and then trying to marry that up with how I see it."

His fingers tightened a fraction. "Then we'll work on showing her that this is real for us." He brought me closer and pressed his lips to mine in a slow, drugging kiss. The time for talking was over, it seemed, with his lips lingering and treasuring mine with one soft kiss after another.

We parted wordlessly so he could remove the remaining clothes he wore. Marcus got the lube and condom, and I waited silently as he came back and lay on his back in the centre of the bed. Our gazes met, and there were no words needed. He often called me beautiful, but to me, he was the truly beautiful one.

I crawled between his parted thighs and bent forward to swallow his cock, wanting him to share how he often made me feel…loved. The silk encased steel slid over my tongue as I sucked him deep. The taste of his precum tempted me to keep tasting. Licking my way up his shaft until my lips popped off, his groan was music to my ears, so I repeated the move several more times until he was gasping and moaning.

"I don't want to come this way," he rasped.

I grabbed the lube and coated my fingers, his nostrils flaring as I raised my hand, going behind me to stretch myself, too impatient to let him do it.

"Let me see."

My cock jerked, a drip of precum hung from the tip, drawing Marcus's gaze as he licked at his lips. Using the lube-free hand, I swiped a finger over the tip of my cock, shuddering as I brought my finger to Marcus's lips. He sucked my finger in between his warm, wet lips. His tongue slid over my finger, the simple action way more erotic than I'd have suspected. A wave of pleasure went through me, right down to my cock.

His eyes glittered as they slit while his tongue made a meal of my finger. The deep moan that came from him tickled my finger, increasing my need. The digit was released, and I twisted wordlessly, so my arse was facing Marcus. Spreading my thighs, I pried open my arse cheeks and slid my lubed fingers down the crease of my arse. A growl came from the head of the bed as I slowly circled my hole, making it slick. The nerve endings zinged with pleasure, and I became impatient for more.

Arse play was something I'd done in private many times. In the past, if one of the other guys I'd been with had asked me to do this, I wasn't sure I'd have been confident enough. With Marcus, it was wholly different.

His hands took hold of my hips. "Push a finger in, stretch that tight little hole for me."

A blush of heat rode up my chest, but I did as he asked. I groaned at the burn as I pushed one finger deep into my arse.

"That's it, so beautiful, show me how much you want me. Ride your finger."

Perspiration sheened my body as I rode one, two, and then three fingers to Marcus's constant encouragement. My cock dripped down between my spread thighs, onto the cover beneath.

"Look at you, so sexy. I'm going to confess that I've wanked off several times to the image of your arse in those little orange pants you wore at the fashion show." One of his hands moved to stroke my arse cheek as I rose and fell on my fingers. Next, his fingers bumped into mine, then a finger ran around my lubed hole. I gasped and cried out in pleasure at the pressure that came from him, stretching me as he pushed a finger into my arse next to mine. I panted, the burn feeling so good. I didn't think about stopping, not when it felt so good.

"Ride our fingers, honey," Marcus rasped sexily.

I threw my head back, gasping for breath as I bounced on our joint fingers, the fullness and stretch undermining my control. I wheezed while trying to string a sentence together. "I'm gonna...come if we...don't stop."

His chuckle was more than a little wicked, but the hand holding my hip stopped me from moving. "Take out your fingers."

He removed his as I took mine out of my arse reluctantly. The emptiness left me mewling, but a second later, I was flat on my back, and Marcus was hovering over me, cloaking his cock. His predatory gaze held mine, and his fingers shook as he lubed his cock. Then, he was pressing his erection against my slick hole. The heat warming my sensitive skin, I held my breath at the wild light in his eyes.

His hips moved back a fraction, the clench of his jaw the only warning as he pushed in deep and fast. The air left my body in a breathy cry, my arse clasping down tightly on Marcus's shaft. Pleasure flooded through me as the eyes staring at me glittered with unrestrained need.

"Hold on," he gritted out.

I'd barely got my arms around his neck before he pulled back and slammed in deep and hard. The care he'd always taken in the past, that part of him seemed incapable of holding back as he set a brutal pace. I'd never felt more owned or precious in my life. That I'd made this man crazy was the biggest fucking turn-on.

Our gazes never wavered. My heart hammered against his as we moaned in unison. His hair was stuck to his face, deep lines appearing around his mouth as he bared his teeth. "Fuck, I love you so god damn much."

The declaration somehow was the switch to my overloaded feelings, and my cock jerked between us, cum shooting from me onto Marcus's muscled stomach. My arse clamped tightly on his cock, and he cried out, his eyes slamming shut while his hips became uncoordinated.

My arse filled with heat as the condom caught Marcus's cum. Long seconds later, his sweaty, heaving chest collapsed against me while his head landed on the pillow next to mine. His body gave several little shudders before he lay panting, his breath tickling my neck.

"You were a beast," I croaked out past my dry throat.

It took a second before he lifted his head. "Is that good or bad?" There was nothing in his voice to indicate what he was thinking, but his body had tensed.

A big grin spread over my face. "Good, though I'm sure my arse will be complaining later. Although no arse can talk, it's more a feeling, though who says an arse can feel? Though it must feel because I can feel you right now. The word is confusing. It has too many..." I shut up when the figure on top of me started to shake uncontrollably.

When he appeared to get control of himself, Marcus pushed his face into my neck. "Fin, you are the best thing that ever happened to me."

Oh!

CHAPTER TWENTY- SEVEN

Marcus

The happy, smiley man who had been chatting about the logistics of moving in together disappeared the moment we'd picked up Elise.

Shit, why had I thought this was a good idea?

Fin stared out the window, his hands clasped together in his lap, not once looking in my direction in the last ten minutes. Should I have kept quiet about exactly where we were going for lunch? I scratched at my eyebrow.

Elise made the odd comment as we passed through the reasonably quiet streets of London, but she didn't try and engage either of us in a conversation. Was it me that was the issue? Or was this to do with the fight she'd had with Fin?

I swallowed a sigh and decided not to try and fill the silence. For the first time, I wondered if I'd miscalculated what was about to happen. Last night, after we'd made love, we'd lain for hours talking. Initially, about the images in my dark room that he'd made me go down and retrieve for him to look at. Fortunately, he'd only laughed at the sheer amount I'd taken and hadn't mentioned that I'd been maybe a smidge inappropriate at the fashion show.

After that, he'd brought up the charities Griffin had mentioned. I'd taken the time to explain a little about what the foundation did. All my attempts at playing it down hadn't worked. Fin had cried and hugged me, resulting in more lovemaking, which had kept us up till four am. We'd eventually fallen asleep wrapped in each other's arms, and I'd never felt happier in my life.

I reached out and placed a hand over Fin's and gave it a gentle squeeze. The smile he offered didn't hide his nerves. I worked on conveying that everything was going to be all right, even though I wasn't super confident of exactly how things would pan out when our mothers met.

When I made the next turn, Fin shifted in his seat. "Where are we going?"

"For lunch," I jested, in the hopes of getting a smile as I glanced at him quickly. The frown that followed left me second-guessing myself. "To my mum's. I mentioned it last night."

"You did?" His eyes widened, the uncertainty there for me to see. The look he cast into the back of the car while he worried his lower lip between his teeth knotted my stomach.

"I did. We'd just, erm well, you know last night." Floundering a little, I couldn't ascertain if he actually remembered because it was in the early hours of the morning. "You want to meet my mum, don't you, Elise?" I glanced in the rear view mirror and swallowed hard enough I could hear the gulp. Elise's mouth was drawn into a tight line.

The longer Elise remained quiet, the more the man in the seat next to me fidgeted. "Is there a problem?" I was compelled to ask, knowing both Fin and Elise would be honest.

"It would have been nice to be informed before I'd gotten in the car that we were meeting your mother." There was an unmissable sharpness to her tone.

"Mum, it's nice that Marcus wants us all to get to know each other." This was followed by a very unladylike snort that got Fin twisting in his seat to glance into the back of the car. "Don't you want to meet Wendy?"

"A little warning would have been nice. I could have prepared something to bring with me," she scolded.

If I'd not been driving, I'd have hunched at her comment. Fin, on the other hand, when I caught his expression, looked relieved. "We can stop at a shop and buy something, maybe some flowers?"

I nodded. "That I can do. I'm sorry Elise, I never thought—"

"That's obvious. Next time, a little warning would be appreciated."

I breathed a little easier at the suggestion there'd be a second time, though I wasn't sure she'd still feel that way after seeing where I was raised.

Flowers sat in Fin's lap thirty minutes later when I pulled through the gates and did my best to pretend I'd not heard the sharp inhale from the back of the car. Parked up, the door to the front of the house opened before we'd even got out of the car. One look at my mother, and I could see she'd dressed for battle. The long flowing dress in pastels skimmed her ankles and clasped her slim waist, and the vee neckline revealed smooth, tanned skin. The jewellery was minimal, a thin gold chain my dad had bought her before he'd died and her wedding band. The smile was one I'd seen countless times. It was her 'don't fuck with me' look.

Elise got out of the car first. I couldn't see her expression, but her posture was anything but relaxed, her shoulders remaining fixed in one position. "Hurry up," Fin hissed through his teeth as he scrambled to release his seatbelt and exit the car.

I sucked in a deep breath and prayed I'd not just made the biggest mistake of my life.

As I got out of the car, I could hear Elise. "The carbon emission from owning such a house is extremely detrimental to the environment."

Fuck!

The Botox left it hard to determine exactly what Mum was thinking as her hand swept wide. "The house has many aspects to it that cater to supporting the environment. I can show you around so you can see what I've done if you like." There was a challenge in her tone, and I knew full well that Elise didn't miss it.

Fin sure as hell hadn't. He flinched, and I slung my arm around his waist, speaking low so no one would overhear. "It's going to be fine."

He pressed against my side, his brows disappearing under his choppy fringe as he glanced up. "You think?"

I kissed his furrowed brow. "Trust me."

An hour later, I wasn't sure if I wanted to kick my arse or congratulate myself. Mum and Elise had disappeared twenty minutes ago, after a heated debate on the pros and cons of creating power through the use of wind turbines. Crestwell Holdings had plans to erect a hundred turbines to assess their viability in generating enough electricity to make creating more wind farms worthwhile. Mum had taken Elise to show her the plans. The quick wink she'd bestowed on me when no one was looking had reduced my stress level from a ten to about an eight. The man next to me, who'd never stopped fidgeting, ensured it remained a little too high for my liking.

Out of all of us, Mum appeared to be the one enjoying herself. I got the impression Elise was still trying to make up her mind about us.

Fin glanced nervously at the door. "Do you think they'll come back soon? I'm starving." He slapped at his forehead, his eyes widening. "Mum's vegan, did you know that? I can't remember if I told you. She's very fussy when it comes to food. This is such a bad idea. She'll kick up a fuss, and Wendy won't want us to come back." His face visibly paled as he spoke.

I took hold of his now icy cold hands and clasped them tightly in mine. "Mum has asked the chef to make a buffet-style lunch, so there'll be lots of options to pick from. I'm sure there will be plenty of green stuff for her to munch on."

A bubble of laughter, which I wasn't convinced wasn't hysteria, followed as Fin's gaze went back to the door before returning to me. "That could work as long as the meat isn't anywhere near the things she'll eat."

Seeing he was going to carry on, I swooped down and pressed my lips to his. A few seconds later, he melted against me and moaned. Releasing his hands, I brought mine up to stroke his face. "Relax, Mum has it all under control," I murmured before deepening the kiss.

The sound of laughter pulled us apart. Fin looked a little dazed as both mums appeared through the door, looking like the best of friends. I took hold of Fin's hand. "Has Mum bored you senseless with all the details."

"They're anything but boring," Elise enthused as she took a seat on the sofa opposite us. She was rough and ready, dressed in hard-wearing trousers and a manly looking shirt, whereas my mother was styled and polished. That said, there were similarities about them, which I picked up as I listened to her converse knowledgeably about the plans, and on the impact versus the benefits of this kind of natural power.

There was no chance to join the discussion, with my mother chiming in to challenge some of what Elise said. Fin's head moved as if he was watching a tennis match.

I chuckled, drawing Fin's gaze.

"They're enjoying themselves." His wide eyes looked a little disbelieving.

I nodded.

Mum glanced at the mantle clock. "Lunch should be laid out for us now." She got up, and we all followed. As we entered the dining room, Mum gave Elise a warm smile. "We're having a buffet-style lunch. If there's anything extra you want, just ask."

The built-in warming cabinet that went along the back wall, as well as the serving counters, were all full of dishes. Fin muttered something I didn't quite catch, but his expression was full of relief.

Elise smacked her lips together. "This all looks very nice. Did you do this?"

Fin tensed.

There was laughter from my mother before she answered. "Ask Marcus about my abilities in the kitchen. They've never been good."

I winked at everyone. "No one wants Mum anywhere near the kitchen, especially if you're hungry."

Fin's stomach rumbled, and everyone laughed. After that, things seemed to be much more relaxed. The conversation was, in the main, between Mum and Elise, which seemed to suit both me and Fin. It was only when we'd returned to the lounge room to have coffee that things went a little pear-shaped.

The conversation somehow came around to Fin and what he'd be doing after uni.

Mum reached for her coffee cup and smiled at Fin. "Have you decided whether you're going to take the job with Marcus?"

CHAPTER TWENTY- EIGHT

Fin

I t was a struggle to swallow. Wendy's face revealed nothing as before, making it impossible to tell if the question had been asked for any other reason than just general interest. I didn't dare look at my mum. Marcus pressed his leg a little more firmly against mine.

"I...yes."

Marcus chuckled, whereas Wendy's brow, I was sure, maybe moved a millimetre. "Yes, you've decided?"

Once more, I didn't look at Mum as I struggled to find some of the words that normally liked to tumble out of my mouth without permission. "I'm taking the job, and

I'm moving in with Marcus." I rolled my eyes to the ceiling. Why had I added that on?

"What? You never mentioned this yesterday." Mum's cup rattled in its saucer as she placed it down on the small coffee table to her left.

"We only talked about it last night," Marcus answered, his voice as smooth as silk. "I was planning to ask him on Friday, but instead, we talked about the concerns Fin raised in regard to the level of responsibility attached to the job I've offered him."

Immediately she sat forward. "Fin is a very responsible person and more than capable," she snapped angrily.

Marcus's grin was...*smug* as he nodded. "He is, and that's why I want him to take on this particularly important job. He understands what I want to achieve with my pictures." Marcus got up and strode over to the large bookcase built into the wall, returning with a book I recognised. He offered it to Mum. "This book is good, but with the research Fin's been doing for me and his narration of the images, the next book is going to be amazing."

Mum remained quiet and flicked through the pages of the book I'd memorised to heart as Marcus returned to the seat next to me and took my clammy hand. Wendy smiled at us both, though I could only tell because her eyes were alight with warmth. Silence seemed the best option until Mum raised her head, her attention focused on me.

"The first image," I said. "Can you feel the old woman's pain and her joy as she holds her husband's hand as he lays dying? I can. Marcus's ability to transport you beyond the picture and into the moment is special. I want to help give another depth to those images, so people understand the history that comes with them. Marcus has done so many amazing things, like the foundation he set up to help those affected by war, that have lost some much. He uses his talent and his money to highlight and help those suffering. It's important to me that his work is valued by the world and that future generations will look back and hopefully not make the same mistakes. What Marcus does matters."

Wendy sniffed. "Well said." Her eyes sheened with tears.

"Oh, I'm sorry. I didn't mean to make you cry."

She held up her hand. "Don't apologise for seeing how wonderful my son is, for being able to see the heart of him." Her gaze moved to Elise. "You've raised an extraordinary young man. I'm so pleased he loves my son the way he deserves to be. The same goes for Marcus. He adores your son, Elise. I hope you'll accept him into your family as I accept Fin into mine."

It was Mum's turn to sniff, only hers didn't sound as dignified as Wendy's. The air remained trapped inside me as I waited for her response and for it to sink in that I was being accepted.

"Love—"

"Is something that a mother fully understands, don't you agree? Can you remember that first moment you felt the new life growing inside you? I can. It was utterly amazing. Daunting as well, to understand the importance that comes with loving and protecting them. You've done an amazing job with Fin. You must *love* him very much."

Her expression was thoughtful. "Yes, yes I do."

I waited for the 'but' as the seconds lengthened. Mum picked her coffee back up, the book remaining open in her lap. "How are you going to manage the daily commute from Brighton to London? And your part-time job, what about that?"

My breath hissed from between my teeth, part in relief and part in fear. "I quit my job when I offered to look after Marcus because I couldn't manage the commute. Billie couldn't cope alone. She needs someone there to help, and as there are plenty of student's looking for part-time work, I thought it was best to resign." This time, I didn't look at the man on my left, who'd suddenly gone very still.

There was a sort of weird throat noise before Marcus growled. "Fuck! Why didn't you say anything?"

I twisted sideways with a shrug. "It's fine. I wanted to take care of you. That was more important than the money. As long as I'm careful with what I've got saved, it should last until I finish in six weeks' time." The second I registered what I said, I groaned. "Crap, I won't be able to commute. I can't afford the train and tube fair."

There was something in Marcus's expression that made my heart leap against my ribs. He carefully set his cup down, then his hands cupped my face. I struggled not to squirm with both our mums watching.

"I love you." He pressed the softest of kisses to my lips. "You can use my car to commute back and forth to Brighton. Maybe Pippa will give you her course notes on the days you only have one lecture? You could cancel the lease too. That will save you some rent money."

"What—"

He continued like I'd not tried to interrupt him. "I own my house, so you won't need to pay rent, and once I start paying you a wage, you'll be able to contribute to the bills. I'm not going to argue about this, you made decisions without telling me about quitting your job, so you're going to have to suck it up, buttercup." He kissed me again, only this time with a lot more passion, making sure to steal my thoughts.

"Now we've sorted that out, who would like some dessert? We have a berry cheesecake and a chocolate torte," Wendy said.

Marcus didn't seem to be concerned about dessert as his lips tilted against mine, giving me one more kiss.

Early the next morning, I'd driven Marcus's car to Brighton to attend uni, then I'd gone to give notice to my landlord. If I was honest, I was still a little in a daze with how the afternoon had panned out. Mum and Wendy had made plans for lunch the following week. Wendy was particularly keen to get Mum's opinion on the conservation projects the company was funding after Mum had explained she was a freelance consultant in the field of conversation.

Marcus hadn't lost his big arse grin all the way back to his house, and I wasn't sure if that was because he'd got his own way or because of how his mum had handled mine. Wendy's ability to silence Mum on the issue of love had been...illuminating. How had we managed to sway Mum about the job with Marcus? Was it me, Marcus or Wendy who'd helped there? Was it an issue who'd finally swayed her into thinking it was a good idea?

With bubbles of excitement at what the future held tickling my insides, I'd have to say no.

By the time I'd packed up my meagre belongings, it was still early in the afternoon, and I was eager to go and pay Nanna a visit to share my news. Back in the car, I drove to Charlie's house and pulled into the drive. The car that Rachael and Nanna used was sitting at the front door. I parked behind it and got out, a smile spreading over my face as both ladies appeared seconds later through the front door.

"Fin, my boy, what are you doing here? How's Marcus's arse? Is it all fixed from your nursing skills?"

"I don't really have any nursing skills unless you count patience. I think nurses need a lot of that. I needed it with Marcus in the beginning. But now he's all smiles again. The egg sitter really helped."

Nanna barked out a laugh. "The egg sitter, what is that? Sounds like Marcus turned into a chicken so he could sit and keep the eggs warm until they are ready to hatch."

Was that even possible, with Marcus being the weight he was? Surely he'd crush the eggs? I shook my head. "I'm sure that's not feasible, Nanna. The egg sitter is a cushion to help with tailbone pain."

Her gaze went back to the house, her brows merging in the middle of her forehead. "Do you have a link for the egg sitter?"

I tugged out my phone. "Let me see if I can find it and send it to you. Do you need it?"

"No, laddie, don't be daft. It's for Charlie boy. He's been walking funny these last few days since Griffin got back." Her eyes lit up. "I think Griffin has been getting kinky with the BSDM again, if you know what I mean?" She tapped her nose, and Rachael shook her head.

Did she mean BDSM? I didn't ask, unsure whether I wanted her answer. Instead, I sent her the link, hoping that it would help with Charlie's obvious issue.

When her phone pinged loudly in her handbag, she smiled at me. "Now we've sorted that, what brings you here, laddie? Is everything all right?"

"It is. I came on Saturday, only you weren't here. But Griffin was, and he gave me some good advice."

"Griff can be very helpful. He just pretends to be a grump to hide his big heart."

I didn't think he pretended, but as Nanna lived with him, I didn't argue. "And you'll never guess. Well, you can't guess because that wouldn't be fair. Anyway, my mum has seen sense after Marcus arranged lunch for our mum's to meet." I beamed at her. "I'm moving in with Marcus and going to work for him."

"Good for you. I'm glad my little tumble helped." She patted my arm, and I stared at her, open-mouthed.

No. Why would anyone fall on purpose? "You fell on purpose? Oh my! You could have broken something. Shit, Marcus did. Oh, Nanna!"

An impish grin was her reply. "You needed time with Marcus, and I'm sorry he broke his arse. It all worked out at the time, though. Elise required a distraction to give you both time to convince her what a great couple you and Marcus are. Now laddie, do you want to join me and Rachael for afternoon tea. We're going all out and having a cream tea."

"Nanna, you are… words fail me."

She tapped my hand. "There's a first time for everything." She looked about and then whispered, "Just don't let on to Charlie how helpful I was with Marcus. He can get a little techy about such things."

I nodded. She was my friend. "I'll not mention it. Or I'll try, you know sometimes I have a little problem with that, but I'll do my best."

"That's all we can ask for, laddie. Now, are you coming for a cream tea?"

"It's very kind of you. I think I'll have to pass as I need to drive back to London."

"Phooey, no one passes up a cream tea. I'm sure you like a bit of *cream*." She winked at me.

Rachael giggled.

Was she talking about...

A wave of heat rode up my neck, and I worked to keep my thoughts to myself. "Yes, well, that's entirely different, Nanna," I said.

She winked at me. "That it is laddie, that it is."

CHAPTER TWENTY-NINE

Marcus

The last few months had flown by, and today was Fin's graduation. He'd been nervous awaiting his results, but he obtained his masters with flying colours, not that I'd have expected anything else. The way he'd set to work on the book project showed just how much he was capable of.

The room he'd taken over in the house for his research was full of books, papers, and magazines. And that didn't even take into account the shelves of DVDs he'd bought secondhand, all connected to anything history related. The man was more driven than me at times when he got excited, which he seemed to be all the time.

Fuck, if he didn't brighten my world by just being a part of it. The time we'd spent together, if possible, had increased the strength and depth of my feelings for him. Today was a special occasion for him, and for me, it marked our six month anniversary. For me, I'd known what I wanted to do to mark it, so I'd done a little research and paid a visit to a jeweller, one Mum had recommended. I was nervous about Fin's reaction to what I'd made for him. He wasn't a traditionalist, and I wanted a symbol that worked for both of us. The flat square box was hidden inside my jacket, which I'd brought only to keep the box in as it was nearly thirty degrees outside.

We'd woken to a sky that was bright blue as far as the eyes could see. The day was perfect for the planned barbeque that Griffin and Charlie were hosting after the ceremony. Both Charlie and Guy were graduating today as well, and we'd decided to combine the celebrations.

There was also just a tiny, perverse part of me that couldn't wait to see Griffin's reaction to Elise. She'd become a frequent visitor to the house, and we'd found a middle ground somehow or other. There were still times she'd argue black was white and vice versa about the merits of love, but I'd learnt to not engage. It wasn't worth it when it could potentially upset Fin, and that was something I preferred to avoid as it hurt my heart. He was such a sensitive soul.

Elise had unexpectedly become firm friends with Mum, and this, in turn, had given her a kick up the butt about working too hard. The planned holiday she was going on the following week with Jed was just one of the many positive changes I'd seen. Something else I had to be grateful for, with Fin coming into my life.

"Are you going to go and find Fin first?"

I glanced at Mum as the car glided to a stop. She'd offered the use of her limo and driver to collect both me and Elise. Elise, for once, hadn't argued, and it seemed she'd made an effort for the occasion, wearing a dress in pale lemon that made her look very pretty. Jed sat next to Mum, wearing a big smile that hadn't left his face since she'd agreed to go on holiday with him.

"Fin has been a bag of nerves since last night. It's probably best I go and find him while you guys go and find our seats."

She smiled and patted my hand. "That's fine, we can do that. Give Fin a hug from me."

"Will do."

The door opened, and I let Mum and Jed go first. Alone in the car with Elise, I glanced at her. "Can I have a quick word?"

"Of course." The only sign she was worried about was the furrow between her brows.

"I'm planning to propose to Fin today. I'm not seeking your approval, but I'd like it anyway. Fin will only be happy if you are. I love him and want to marry him." It came out more like a croak, but I'd kept it together, which, with the way my heart was beating up into my throat, was about the best I could hope for.

This was met with a prolonged silence that got my palms sweating.

"Fin has never seemed happier, and I know you've played a big part in that. You've given him something I was never able to." Her gaze met mine. "The freedom to really be himself, to know that he's enough just as he is."

A ball lodged right at the back of my throat, and the achy feeling in my eyes left my vision a little blurry. I blinked, swallowed hard and nodded. It was all I was capable of.

"You have my blessing." She got up and pressed a kiss to my cheek, wordlessly getting out of the car.

I blew out a shaky breath. One hurdle down. I lifted my jacket and touched the box. *Please let him say yes.*

I found Fin with Charlie, Guy, Brett, Griffin, Agnes, and Rachael, looking more than a little terrified, dressed in his cap and gown.

"You okay?" I asked, taking hold of one of his hands to squeeze his fingers. "Your mum, mine, and Jed have gone to find our seats."

There was a nod but no other response as Fin glanced to the big doors of the hall the ceremony was being held in. "What if I start talking and can't stop?"

Nudging his shoulder with mine to get him to look at me, I smiled. "And? I love when you can't stop talking. It's sexy."

He blushed while Agnes nodded. "It's what makes you special, laddie. Go in there and knock their socks off."

"That would be very difficult—"

I kissed him to stop the ramble, knowing that he'd only get more nervous when it was announced everyone needed to find their seats. "Go on. I love you."

It took another kiss and a nudge to get him through the doors. I kept my fingers crossed he'd be okay.

Several hours later, we were all at Griffin's, and the party was in full swing. I'd decided to have a couple of glasses of wine to give me some Dutch courage. I'd struggled to find a moment alone with Fin because every time I managed to get him away from one person, another would come to congratulate him. That was great for him, and it was wonderful to see him get all flustered, but not so great for me and the knots forming in my stomach.

"Why are you scowling? Aren't you enjoying the party?" Fin whispered in my ear.

"It's a wonderful party, it's just I'd like five minutes alone with my boyfriend," I said through the side of my mouth while trying to smile at Pippa and the girl she was with, whose name I couldn't remember. A guy standing across the garden with Charlie waved them over, and I released a sigh of relief when they walked off a few seconds later.

Fin's smile grew big and wide, reminding me of the very first time I'd seen him all those months ago at The Worthington. He all but beamed happiness at me. "God, I love you."

His eyes twinkled. "Is that the sixth or the seventh time you've told me today?"

"Whatever the tally, I'm sure it's not nearly enough."

He laughed. "I don't mind. I love hearing you say it." He touched the centre of his chest. "No matter how often you tell me, it gives me a buzzy feeling right here. Do you think it might be giving my heart a little love boost?" He shook his head and laughed at himself.

"I hope so."

His eyes got a little misty. "I do too."

Somehow knowing this was the best moment, I searched in my jacket pocket and pulled out the box. Fin glanced down, and his eyes widened. "What's in the box?"

When his gaze returned to mine, I sucked in a shaky breath. "It's a gift, something to show how much you mean to me, but also to demonstrate a commitment for our future together." I'd been careful with my words, or so I'd thought.

"You're proposing to me," he squealed in a very loud voice, drawing the attention of nearly everyone who stood in the large back garden.

Okay then!

Ignoring everyone around us as best I could, especially with both our mum's attention aimed in our direction, I nodded. Heat I'd swear was from the sun filled my face. "I am."

I glanced about and aimed my jacket at an empty seat a few feet away, uncaring where it landed as I focused back on Fin. My ears buzzed as I lifted the lid to reveal the bracelet nestled inside the box. It was made of recycled sea plastic, something I understood Fin would appreciate. I'd had Mum's jeweller add two rows of black onyx stones. At the two ends, I'd had the jeweller make the clasp something different. It was made up of a tiny book with Fin's name inscribed into the platinum and a camera with my name on it. I'd wanted something that represented us both. "So, Finlo Denning, will you marry me?"

My fingers trembled at the silence that followed as I lifted out the bracelet and tucked the box into my trouser pocket. The beat of my heart resonated through me as I worked to stop hyperventilating while I undid the clasp before holding it out towards him.

His lips quivered, his eyes glistening in the late afternoon sun as he stared at what I was offering him. "Are you sure?"

The lack of ramble said everything. "I've never been more sure about anything," I answered honestly.

There were several sighs and a couple of sniffles, but I didn't take my eyes off the man in front of me.

His quivering smile was beautiful as he held out his wrist. "Yes."

I narrowed the gap between us to put the bracelet around his wrist. "I know a bracelet isn't normally a traditional engagement thing. But when I was thinking about this, I wanted something that would have meaning to us. The camera is me, the book is you. The band is made from recycled sea plastic, and the black onyx is supposed to help promote self-control." There were titters of laughter, and Fin chuckled.

As the bracelet lay against his fair skin, gleaming in the sunlight, I touched it. "It also offers protection, strength, and good fortune. I want all those things for you," I said, emotions thickening my voice.

He removed the gap between us to wrap his arms around my waist. His hands stroked up my back, his focus solely on me. "Thank you, it's beautiful, and I love it." He got up on his tiptoes and brushed his lips against mine.

"But just so you know, I found all those things in you," he whispered.

My heart trembled as I whispered back, "You'll always have them."

EPILOGUE

Fin

It was hard to remain still, but the light was so dim beyond the crack in the curtains. I tried because it had been extremely late when we'd got to bed last night. We'd had a kind of going away party that Wendy had arranged for us.

I'm going on a trip! I resisted pinching myself as I'd already done that and given myself a bruise that I'd then had to explain to Marcus. I sighed.

"You're thinking far too loudly for someone who's supposed to be sleeping," Marcus grumbled as he nuzzled at my neck.

"Is that even possible? I suppose it could be. Otherwise, we wouldn't have all these books on that type of phenomena."

Marcus made a groaning noise as his erection pushed against my backside. "See, talking like that has woken up my other head."

The giggle escaped but then turned to a moan as Marcus rolled his hips, his hand sliding around to take hold of my thickening cock. He kissed his way up the side of my neck. The slick precum helped with the glide of his cock as he pushed it between my thighs. I clamped them tight together, causing Marcus to groan loudly, his breath tickling my skin. He rocked his hips while his hand followed the same motion. On and on, he stroked me, in time to the thrust of his hips, his tongue licking up the side of my throat and stopping at my ear.

"I love you," he whispered while increasing the speed of his hips and the strokes of his hand up and down my cock. The roughness of his palm and the feel of him surrounding me was all I needed to come. I panted as my cock thickened and cum coated Marcus's hand. It didn't take long before cum spread between my clamped thighs, and Marcus's big body repeatedly shuddered against my back.

The sounds of heavy breathing were the only noises in the room for long minutes before Marcus removed his sticky hand from under the cover and laughed. "You got me all dirty. What are you going to do about it?"

"I think you'll find I'm as dirty as you are. What are you going to do about that?"

Before I could register his intention, he was up and smearing his hand over my chest, laughing when he sat back to stare at my cum covered body.

"That's only made it worse," I accused through my own laughter.

"Then I'll have to do something about that. We can't have you all dirty before we go on holiday, can we?" The wicked glint in his eyes got my cock twitching, then the air got stuck in my lungs as he bent forward, his tongue licking my chest clean.

I moaned. "I..." Talking was overrated.

Much later, after Marcus had thoroughly cleaned me with his mouth, we'd showered and dressed in a hurry. Way behind schedule for the pick-up time for the car Marcus had arranged to collect us, I was now in a panic.

"Marcus? Marcus, where are you? Have you finished packing? The car is here to take us to the airport." I rushed up the stairs and tripped at the top, careening into Marcus.

He steadied me, his face alight with humour. He was dressed head to toe in black, looking dark and dangerous. "You do know that if you injure yourself, we won't be going anywhere but to the emergency department?"

"No, we are not. I don't care if I hurt myself. This is my first trip abroad. Nothing is going to stop me from travelling."

Rich laughter followed as Marcus let go of my arms after he'd made sure I was steady. "What if your leg was hanging off?"

There was impish humour sparkling in his eyes that said he was baiting me. It was something he frequently did because he loved to hear me ramble. Like this morning, it had a very odd effect on him. One I'd admit I loved.

Instead of pointing it out, I rolled my eyes at him. Then, unable to stop myself—although to be honest, I didn't try awfully hard because, why would I—I started to ramble. "Why would my leg be hanging off? I don't think tripping up the top stair could result in an injury of that kind. Or could it? No, I can't see it unless there was something to catch your femoral artery on. Erm—"

"I thought you were in a rush to leave," he said around his laughter.

"Oh yes, the driver is here. What was I saying?"

He looked towards the pile of suitcases sat outside our bedroom door. "The bags. I was just bringing them down."

"They're all sorted? I've got the driver to put the camera bags in already as they were downstairs." We'd been planning this trip to Egypt so I could visit the pyramids for the last couple of months. A whole four-week vacation, something I'd never had. Marcus had surprised me on our one year anniversary with several brochures for a number of historical sites I'd mentioned I'd wanted to visit, so I could pick somewhere for my first ever holiday abroad. This, he'd promised me, was the first of many trips.

There'd been no chance to take one before now with the launch of Marcus's book and the two exhibitions he'd signed up for. I'd not minded, not when his new book had been so widely acclaimed.

"Did you put all the books I left out in the suitcase?"

That stopped the laughter and got a sigh in return. "I did. All I can say is, it's a good job we have a private jet or else we'd be going naked on holiday, given normal suitcase weight restrictions."

"What? Weight restrictions? What are you talking about? How can there be weight restrictions? A plane is clearly not light and can manage to get up in the sky—"

His lips pressed against mine, stopping me in the most effective way. A way he and I never seemed to grow tired of. Not a lot had changed since I'd moved in, and yet everything had. Life with Marcus was always full of surprises that made each day, as Nanna called them, "a detour". I never knew where each day would lead, with one exception, Marcus. They all led to him, which was perfect.

The shout from downstairs pulled me from the haze of desire Marcus's kisses always caused. "Shit, the driver. We need to get going."

"That we do. We've our own pictures to create and memories to make. I want fill our hallways with the light and love you've given me." He laid his brow against mine. "It's time to sell the photo's up here. We can give the proceeds to those who need it most. All I need is you."

A smile spread over my lips and my heart skipped a beat. I couldn't have said it better.

This is the last in the Billionaire's Playground...I think lol, but who knows for sure.

Next up from me is Chozen something completely different for me. A dark crime-drama with more twists than Line of Duty...Out September read on for an unedited snippet!

PLAYERS KINGDOM: 2016

My breath came in short gasps as I waited for the man to step forward and inspect me. The pain in my body was no longer what I was worried about, it meant I was alive. The fear of death had become my constant companion as Macintosh told me daily he'd decide on what my fate will be.

"You've trained him well," the nameless man said as his dark soulless eyes ran over my naked body. The suit he wore was expensive. His hair was cropped short and once upon a time I'd have thought he was attractive but I'd learned to look past the outer shell to the man beneath. The eyes didn't lie if you looked close enough you could see the monster lurking underneath the polished exterior. There were so many that wore the mask of deception and they all came to Player's Kingdom in search of the depravity their souls seemed to crave.

The monsters in the stories my mother had read to me as a child were no longer fictional characters but living breathing men who wore suits and pretended that they weren't evil bastards.

As the man stepped closer the overpowering scent of his aftershave filled my nose. I didn't move or twitch, those things weren't permitted. Some days taking a breath was forbidden.

This was my life because that was what Macintosh had made it. He ruled my world, owned me. He'd told me so often I believed him. He'd made sure it was the only thing I could remember. The happy boy that had been snatched off the street, he's long gone. In his place was a robot, one that knew what would happen if those who were playing with me don't get the right reaction. These men were worse than spoilt children because when they lashed they left scars, some that would never heal.

"Of course, he's mine. Aren't you boy?" Macintosh answered, sounding smug. He had every right, he's given me what he called his 'special treatment'. I shut down the negative thoughts, thinking only of my safe place. The room in his home that was my cage, but had also become my sanctuary. When I was locked inside no one got to touch me, not even Macintosh.

Doing what was excepted, I gave the merest of nods maintaining the perfect pose. My arms didn't tremble, trained to understand that my master wouldn't want that.

A cold hand ran over my chest and I sank into the place inside my mind that these men couldn't touch. The place I went often in the hopes one day I'd never come back.

"Beautiful," the man whispered as he trailed his nails over the scared flesh on my chest.

The skin covering my body showed that I was not the one in charge, that no matter what the internet said about submission, I had no power here.

"Remember he's not for sale. My sub is special." Macintosh reiterated and suddenly the room filled with a tension that I recognised would not end well.

The man in front of me didn't remove his hand, in fact his nails dug into my flesh deep enough blood dripped down my chest. I breathed slow and even, the mantra already starting to play over in my head. *Don't move. Don't move. Don't Move.*

"Weren't you the one to invite me to play?" The man's hard eyes moved from Macintosh to me. "He's perfect. And now you've shown him to me, do you think I wouldn't want to sample his delights?"

"That maybe so, but you forget yourself. I've already shown you the selection we have on offer for you. My sub is not part of the deal." Macintosh remained sitting causally on the chair, but I knew better. He could strike as fast as a panther. His eyes glittered with warning as he continued. "The power you think you have doesn't extend over my world. Or have you forgotten this?" Macintosh's voice was dark and dangerous as it rippled out like the leather of his favourite whip.

It was a struggle to keep my pose with the dominate battle happening right in front of me. My jaw ached as Macintosh slowly stood to his impressive six-four height. He was taller than the other man but they both appeared as big as each other in the confines of the room. The power battle was real and extremely dangerous. I've come to understand that these high powered men didn't care who the casualties were in the fallout.

My heart thudded painfully against my ribs while I struggled to show no sign of distress and draw any attention to myself when the tension in the room continued to thicken. The four men stood behind Macintosh watched with lazy interest. The bulges beneath their suit jackets wasn't fat. They didn't seem in the least bit concerned about what could potentially happen next, while I was way too close to both men.

The unknown man puffed out his chest, his eyes narrowed to slits. "I forget nothing. It's you whose memory is short." A hand swept the massive playroom designed for any kind of BDSM play. The walls were white and held multiple brackets for the equipment that hung macabrely against the white backdrop.

"Your large mansion, your businesses, they are only possible because I allow it and you need to remember that."

Before anyone could react the guy took hold of my throat and his large fingers squeezed shutting off my oxygen supply. His gaze still on Macintosh who'd not moved. "I own you and this sub." As if to prove his point he squeezed harder, I shut out the world around me. The pain clawed at me, but to give and break pose was forbidden.

If I survived this then the punishment for disobeying would be far worse. The fingers dug in hard enough that the edges of my mind became fuzzy. Was this it, was this man going to succeed where others had failed?

"Let him go, *now.*" Deadly intent filtered past the buzzing as I started to struggle to maintain my perfect pose. Tears leaked out the corners of my eyes. The defeat came in crushing waves as my hands came up to claw at the hands that didn't let go.

There was a shout, then the sound of an explosion as liquid hit my face. The seconds seemed to pass in slow motion as I started into soulless eyes. A river of dark red ran over his face as the hand around my throat fell away when he collapsed towards me. His misshapen head looked like an exploded melon, the brain and bone was revealed for all to see. The coppery scent overpowering as blood dripped into my own mouth as I opened it to scream.

The fear of retribution overridden by the sight, the smell, the taste and feel of death on my skin.

His body pressed against mine, the dead weight taking me with him to the floor. The loud thud and pain as we landed on the wood hardly penetrated past the terror as I was immersed in death. Pinned to the floor, the screams started and I wasn't sure they'd ever stop.

Dead.

Dead.

Dead.

OTHER BOOKS BY THE AUTHOR

Standalone
When Fake Changed Everything
Christmas beyond Christmas
The Elves and the Bondage Daddy (Grim and
Sinister Delights Book 5)
Sweet Haven

Series
The Potters Creek Series
A Christmas Wish (book one)

The App Series
The App: Daddy kink (book one)
The App: Littles (book two)
The App: Puppy play (book three)

The Flamingo Bar Series
Always More (book one)
The Little Side of Me (book two)
3 Is the Magic Number (book three)

La Trattoria Di Amore Series
Puzzle Pieces (book one)
Dominated but not Subdued (book two)
Made to Submit (book three)

The Playroom Series
Mine, Body and Soul: Part One
Mine, Body and Soul: Part Two

Mine, Body and Soul: Part Three
Ferron's Journey: Damaged Part One (book four)
Ferron's Journey: Hidden Part Two (book five)
Ferron's Journey: Revelation Part Three (book six)
Mine, Body and Soul Trilogy
Ferron's Journey Trilogy

Dark River Stone Collective Series
The Light Beneath the Dark (Book One)
When Darkness Turns to Light (Book Two)

The Billionaire Playground Series
Property of a Billionaire (Book one)
Reluctant Billionaire (Book two)

The Manx Cat Guardians Series
Where it all Began: Origins (Book 1)
Seeing Beyond the Scars (Book 2)
Destiny Collides Past and Present (Book 3)
Searching for a Soul to Love (Book 4)
The 12 Disasters of Christmas (Book 5)
Laws of Attraction (Book 6)
The Teacher's Boy (Book 7)
Boxset

Audio Books
Mine, Body and Soul, Part One: The Playroom Series
Mine, Body and Soul, Part Two: The Playroom Series

Mine, Body and Soul, Part Three: The
Playroom Series
Daddy Kink: The App (book one)
Always More: The Flamingo Bar (book one)
When Fake Changed Everything
Ferron's Journey: Damaged Part One
Ferron's Journey: Hidden Part Two
Ferron's Journey: Revelation Part Three

ABOUT THE AUTHOR

Eccentric cake lover who has a passion for words of all kinds. I'm Jayne or JP, I live in the Isle of Man. A tiny place in the Irish sea where all the magic happens. I'm a confessed bookaholic and if I'm not writing I love to snuggle with a book or two...if you catch my drift.

If you're interested in keeping up to date, then I've a few places you can do that and there listed below. If you would like to give me any feedback or just have any questions, go ahead and friend me on Facebook, and I would be happy to answer anything. Well, almost anything. I hope you enjoyed this book and if you would also like to leave a review, then I would love to read your thoughts.

Thank you for being a part of my dream.